Witch Princess

also by

DOROTHY JOHNSON

Farewell to Troy

Witch Princess

DOROTHY JOHNSON

Illustrated by Carolyn Cather

HOUGHTON MIFFLIN COMPANY BOSTON

The author is grateful to Professor John G. Watkins, University of Montana, for information about hypnotism.

SECOND PRINTING   C

This book is dedicated to

LEE HUMMEL

a blonde, like Medea, but no witch

1

In this city, where I will spend the rest of my life, I am a foreigner but not a stranger any more. I remember sometimes another home, far away, very far from here. I remember the dreadful journey from that home to this one.

And I remember the witch princess, Medea, beautiful and strange, a king's daughter and priestess to the Dark Goddess.

I shall never see Princess Medea again. The sea is between us, and fate divides us too. But I remember my lady Medea, and I know that she remembers me.

My parents named me Daphne, but sometimes my mother laughed and called me Themis, for the goddess of divine order, because I tried so hard to keep the younger children obedient and busy at whatever tasks they could be expected to perform.

There was not much laughter in our hut, four days' journey from the royal palace in Colchis. There were many mouths to feed — eight of us children by the time I was twelve, when I went to live with the King's daughter, Medea.

My father had a few sheep, and he guarded flocks in

the mountains for other men, keeping off the wolves and other beasts. He had a little land, and on it my mother and we children raised grain for our bread, and cabbages and beans. There was never enough wool for clothing to keep us all warm in winter and never enough food after snow came. But we did not know anyone who was always warm and never hungry.

Often I wonder what has become of my parents. Now I live so far away that there is no hope of ever hearing from home. I am never hungry, never cold, and I would like to share my good fortune with my family back home, but that is not fated.

I have a strange and frightening gift. Sometimes — but only sometimes — I can foresee and farsee.

2

The first time it happened, I was about six years old. In the night I began to cry, and my mother comforted me, but I went on sobbing and said, "Father is fighting wolves!"

She thought this was only a bad dream, of course, but she worried. The next morning she asked, "Is your father still fighting wolves?" and I answered, "No, he drove them off, but they killed a ewe."

That seemed like a little girl's made-up story. But when my father came back to our hut, she asked him, and he said it had really happened. They were both afraid then, and to keep harm away from me they sacrificed to the goddess Hecate that night after the moon came up. They burned a cup of grain on our little altar in the willows down by the spring and made me sprinkle a few drops of wine on the threshold.

My mother kissed me and said, "Now the Dark Goddess will keep us safe. Maybe you are a farseer. My grandmother had the gift."

Sometimes thereafter I knew what was happening far away. But it was not until later that I could tell what would happen in the future. That is an uncomfortable gift, to be a paragnost, one who knows beyond wisdom. You cannot always tell whether you are foreseeing something that hasn't happened yet or farseeing what is happening when you see it.

It was in my tenth summer that I saw men coming with laden donkeys and mentioned it to my mother.

"There are three men coming," I said, "and one of them wears fine clothing. The others are slaves. They are cold in the snow."

3

She stared. "But it is summer! We haven't begun to reap the grain. How can there be snow?"

She fretted about the matter for several days and talked it over with a neighbor woman and said often, "I wish my husband were here. He'd know what to do."

"I know what I'd do if a child of mine told such stories," the neighbor said. "Thanks to all the gods that none of them ever did! But if one had, about strangers coming — well, I'd talk to the headman of our village, because it might mean danger. Unless, of course, Daphne made it all up."

All I wanted by that time was for the matter to be forgotten. But my mother made me wash myself clean, and she braided my hair neatly, and we went to see the headman.

We found him cross because his wooden plough was broken, but he listened to the story my mother told.

"What did the men look like?" he asked, scowling.

"They were leading two loaded donkeys," I remembered, "and they wore good warm mantles, even the slaves. They have some animals bigger than donkeys — a kind I never saw before. They ride them. There should be another man with them, their leader, but he is lost and they are worried."

The headman stroked his beard. "Tax collectors!" he exclaimed. "Who else comes wearing fine clothes? And with horses? Coming in winter, when we don't expect them!

"We don't have our possessions hidden then. The flocks are down here, not up in the mountains. Those

4

men can count sheep and goats, let me tell you, and measure grain and olive oil at a glance — if they see it. But we can hide those things even in winter, now that we're warned.

"We are not opposed to paying the King his rightful tax, but we think the collectors keep too much for themselves, so it never reaches the palace storerooms."

My mother asked humbly, "You believe the child, then? You think she is a foreseer?"

"Maybe. The Princess Medea is. Or so they say. Of course I don't know any fine people like the Princess.

"We'll make some changes in the way we store our produce, and next winter we'll find out whether Daphne has the gift.

"If she does," he added, "maybe the Princess will want to know about her. She is a priestess of Hecate, as her older sister used to be, and understands all sorts of magic and witchcraft."

The strange thing about the gift I had is that it is useful only for other people. There was never any warning for me personally, or promise of good things, either. I could farsee and foresee — sometimes, only sometimes — what was happening or would happen to other people, but not for myself.

The summer went along as usual. My friend Electra and I took care of our younger brothers and sisters and did a great deal of spinning — and a great deal of chattering, as girls will. Making yarn with distaff and spindle keeps one's hands occupied but does not still one's tongue. If it did, my father once remarked, there would

5

be no yarn to weave into cloth and everybody would have to wear goatskins — as he did when he was guarding the flocks in the woods.

We had school every morning, all the younger children of the village, under a shade tree. School was mostly religious training, and our teacher was an old man who was a priest of Prometheus. The old man would have tears in his eyes — and so did we — when he told us about Prometheus, chained to a rock on a mountain peak with a great bird pecking at his liver every day, because the younger but greater god, Zeus, was punishing him for keeping a secret.

Prometheus had brought mankind the gift of fire, which Zeus did not want us to have because we were so worthless.

"Prometheus' mountain is over that way," our teacher told us, pointing. "Some day he will be freed by a hero who will die in his place. Prometheus is divine and cannot die. The meaning of this, children, is that all suffering comes to an end. This is the promise without which we could not endure."

Then we would chant a prayer of thanks to Prometheus and one of supplication to Zeus, asking that the day of deliverance might come soon.

We learned about the goddess Hecate, too, whom even powerful Zeus honored. She could give to mortals any gift she wished, or she could withhold anything. She was the three-part goddess of the moon and of darkness. When dogs howled at night, they spoke to Hecate.

It was all very puzzling, that we must worship Prometheus, who had defied great Zeus, and worship Zeus, too, although he was sometimes cruel. The old man told us gently, "There are many things about religion that children cannot understand. Or grownups, either. I have been learning all my life."

When winter came, our village was ready. On a cold day, a messenger came trudging through the snow to our hut to say that the headman wanted to see me. I was terrified, but my father went with me.

Three men were in the headman's house, shivering. The best-dressed one had his feet in a big bowl of snow, and one of his slaves was rubbing them to get the frostbite out. Lord Frozen Feet kept saying, "Ouch, not so hard!"

The headman told my father, "The noble tax collector — this lord's father — is lost somewhere. He was separated from the others in a snowstorm. Can your little girl tell where he is?"

My father answered, "Once she knew where the baby was when nobody else could find him. She knew just by handling his wooden doll. Have you anything that the missing lord has touched?"

"His sash of ceremony," said Lord Frozen Feet. He beckoned to the other slave, who brought it from the pack and handed it to me. The sash was so beautiful, finely woven of bright-colored threads, that I couldn't stop staring at it.

"Come, come, girl," the headman chided. "Hurry up."

The farseeing was easy when I held the sash of ceremony.

"He is a big man with a black beard," I said. "He is sitting by the fire in a farmer's hut, and he is angry at being separated from these other men, but he is not hurt. He is only hungry. The farmer has little food, but he shares what he has."

"Thanks be to all the gods!" exclaimed Lord Frozen Feet. "And where is this hut?"

"He turned left in the storm when you were passing through a grove, just before you came to a river," I said.

"I remember! I remember the grove — and the blinding storm, and what a time we had at that river! I vow by Hermes the guide of souls I'll never venture out on another winter expedition. And neither will my father, I'll wager."

The headman solemnly winked at my father and told the tax collector's son, "We'll do all we can to make you comfortable, sir, but we have not much to offer. The harvest was poor — the olive trees did not bear this year — we lost sheep and goats — "

"I know, I know," Lord Frozen Feet said, half smiling. "I've heard all that before. It's an old story. But you are as hospitable as a king, and I am grateful. I believe the little girl. We'll find my father. As a reward to you and your village, we will remit your taxes for the whole year!"

Two days later, when he left, all the villagers came out to wave good-by. One of our neighbors remarked, "That was the first time I ever liked a tax collector!"

But I didn't like him. He was going to tell the people in the palace about me, and maybe I would have to go there to live.

Our village buzzed with the news, and so many women came to talk to my mother that she could hardly get her work done. But of course when she had to sit down to be polite to callers, her hands were always busy with distaff and spindle, spinning yarn from wool.

We did not know very much about the capital city where the King lived. One very old man had been there once, in his youth, and he was full of stories, but nobody really believed them all.

He was the only one still alive who had actually seen the great hero from our village who had gone to the city long ago to tell the king of our famine. His name was Orthrus, and because our people were starving after a poor harvest, he had struggled through the winter snow to plead for food from the King. Orthrus died after he reached the city, but the King sent soldiers with grain and dried fish, and half the people in the village lived to see the spring.

Every spring we held a religious festival in honor of Orthrus and sacrificed to his spirit in the world below. But his body was not where our altar was, because he had died in the city.

There was no reason why anyone from our village should go to the city. There was another village a few miles from ours, and the people traded their produce back and forth, but we had nothing worth taking clear to the city, and there were robbers on the road.

So most of what was said in our village about the palace was rumor, based on what people overheard the tax collector and his servants say when they came once a year.

The King had a daughter named Medea, they told, who was skilled in charms and spells. She was the priestess of the goddess Hecate and very fearsome, some said. Others didn't believe this; they said she was young and beautiful and had twelve chosen maidens for her companions. Perhaps I would be one of them.

My family worried, and so did I. The next summer the tax collector did not come, because he had promised not to. But the next year he did, and I wanted to run and hide in the forest, but my mother wouldn't let me. She talked to the tax collector herself and came back, very much relieved.

"You won't have to go with the tax lords," she told me. "They travel slowly because of the pack animals and the goats and sheep they have to drive. A party of soldiers will come especially for you, because the Lady Medea really wants you for one of her companions."

Medea was a farseer and a foreseer, and that was why she wanted me.

"Her girls live very comfortably," my mother reported. "Each of them is especially skilled in something and teaches all the others. The Lady Medea is kind, and she gives them fine dowries, so they marry well. You must go, Daphne."

Then she hugged me, and we both cried.

My best friend, Electra, was my own age. We spent all the time together that we could while we waited for the soldiers. I looked after my littlest brother and she watched over her littlest sister, and of course our hands were not idle, but we could spin while talking and guessing and dreaming about what the city would be like and whether we would ever meet again. Now I know we never will.

One day while we were sitting in the shade with the babies we heard much shouting in the village.

"They've come for you," Electra said.

We picked up the babies and ran to see.

"Six soldiers!" Electra gasped. "Do they think you are so big and strong that you will fight them?"

They were big and strong, riding those big animals called horses. The men wore leather helmets and body armor of leather, and each carried two short spears fastened to his saddle. They had bows and quivers of arrows, too.

My mother came running. "It is a guard of honor for you, Daphne. And you must see the fine gifts they brought, some for our family and some for the whole village!"

"Are they buying me?" I asked, frightened. "Will I be a slave?" For we had heard that in the city there were slaves and that the men who came with the tax collectors were slaves.

"No, these are gifts from the Princess, the captain says. You will go tomorrow."

Electra said, "I have a farewell gift for you," and I replied, "I have a gift for you, too."

When we parted the next day, we exchanged our treasures. Mine to her was a necklace of little shells, precious because our village was so far from the sea. Someone in my family long ago had got them, and I wore the necklace only for great religious festivals.

Her gift to me was a carved wooden bowl, lovingly polished and long used. It was a family treasure, said to have belonged to the hero Orthrus.

All the village gathered for the parting, except the men who were in the mountains with the flocks. A boy ran

11

to get my father and stayed with the flocks while he came down to bid me farewell.

The captain of the soldiers made a little speech:

"The Princess Medea, daughter of King Aeetes, sends these gifts to honor the village and the family of Daphne, who has been chosen as one of her companions. We will escort Daphne to the city and make the journey as comfortable as possible."

My mother cried out, "We'll never see her again!"

The captain answered gruffly, "Nonsense, Madame. In a few years you will come to her wedding. When one of the girls marries, the Princess sees to it that her parents are brought to the city. She has done it three times now. And her girls marry well, because of the advantages they have, being educated in the palace, and because of the fine dowries she gives them."

"That may be," my mother said, and kissed me. "Be kind to the Lady Medea."

A strange thing to say! "How can I be kind to a princess?" I asked. "I'm nobody."

"Everyone needs kindness, even those in high places. Sometimes it is all we have to give."

The time came when Medea needed my kindness. And it was, as my mother had said, all I had to give.

"And here," the captain said, "is a present from the Princess for little Daphne herself." He beckoned, and a soldier led up a fine gray donkey. The captain handed me the neck rope, smiling. "He's for you to ride, because you're not accustomed to big horses."

The donkey was a fine little beast, soft to stroke and

with a sweet, stupid face. He nuzzled my arm and breathed on me.

"If he is mine," I said, "then I give him to my mother. She needs him to carry firewood from the forest."

"But the palace is four days from here, traveling horseback!" the captain exclaimed. "Do you expect to walk all the way?"

"He was my donkey," I said stubbornly. "I will thank the Princess."

I would rather not remember any more about that parting.

Of course they didn't make me walk to the city. I rode behind the captain or one of the soldiers on a great, tall horse. I hung on tight, because it is farther to fall off a horse than off a donkey, and horses travel much faster.

I had with me everything that could be spared for me to take, wrapped in a small, mended shawl. My mother had given me a pretty woven band to hold back my hair, and my father had carved a comb from wood. I had a drinking cup of wood and a small piece of woolen cloth for a towel. And the precious bowl that was the parting gift of my best friend. I do not have any of these things any more.

2

Every afternoon we stopped to make camp and to let the horses graze. I wanted to help gather wood for the fire, but the captain wouldn't let me.

"Tut!" he said. "How would it look if one of the Princess's young ladies were seen carrying firewood while six strong men sat around doing nothing?"

"Who will see me?" I asked. But he was impressed with the importance of appearances and still refused. The men set up a small tent each night for me — that was proper, they said, and everything had to be done correctly. They carried water and did the cooking — twice we had wild birds, shot by one of the archers. All I did was clean myself up at the nearest stream and wander around with nothing to do. I had no spinning and no babies to tend, and my hands felt empty and lazy.

On the fourth day, the road became plainer, and we began to pass people on foot, carrying loads on their backs, and people leading loaded donkeys. I had never seen so many people in my life.

"Market day," said the captain. "All the farmers are coming to town to trade their produce. We're near the city now. Halt! Dismount! At ease!"

He took off his helmet and stared at me, scratching his head.

"We'll have to arrange for a proper entry," he said. "There aren't any rules, so we'll have to invent some. It wouldn't look right for the young lady to come in on the back of somebody's saddle like a farm girl."

"I *am* a farm girl, sir," I reminded him.

"Not any more, you aren't. Let me see. We want to look like an honor guard, not a foraging party that's caught a captive."

Finally he decided that he would ride ahead, then I would be on a horse alone, with a mounted man on each side of me, two mounted men behind, single file, and the sixth soldier on foot leading the pack mule that carried the baggage. That soldier grumbled, but the captain growled at him and he was quiet.

The gate guards saluted and let us through — they let all the country people through, too, but without saluting. In a place where two streets crossed, farmers and their wives were sitting on the ground, guarding their little heaps of vegetables or fruit. Some had a squealing pig or a bleating lamb or a few fowls, and everyone was yelling.

"What are they quarreling about?" I asked, frightened.

The man at my right laughed. "They're only trading. A basket of lentils for a dove, or garlic for apples. Surely they do that in your village?"

"We bargain quietly," I answered.

"You're in the big city now," he said. "Things are different here."

They certainly were. I was even afraid of the country

15

people here, although they looked just like the people back home. How much more afraid I would be of the Princess Medea!

Suddenly, as we rode along the street, I had a farseeing. A slim young woman wearing a black robe and a black mantle was leaning against a tree, all alone, with a look of terrible sadness on her face. She began to cry into her hands. Then she was gone.

The palace consisted of many buildings and courtyards, and there were people carrying burdens of various kinds, going about their business. On each side of the main gate there was a bull made of stone, with a bronze head and bronze feet.

The captain lifted me down from my horse and said, "Wait here while I get somebody to look after you.

Good luck, little Daphne. Be happy."

"Thank you for caring for me so kindly, sir," I replied.

I waited, holding my little bundle and wished I could wash the dust off myself and comb my hair. The captain came back with a tall girl who moved regally, with her head held high, and who looked at me without smiling. The captain said, "Here's Daphne," saluted me smiling, and took his men away.

This was a royal girl, from the way she acted, but surely the Princess herself wouldn't come to meet me.

"My name is Rhoda," she said. "I am the Lady Medea's best friend. I have been with her longer than any of the others. Come this way." She wore a pale pink robe, prettily draped and without any patches. "I see you'll have a lot to learn," she remarked over her shoulder. I felt utterly miserable.

She took me to a room with many looms in it, big and small, but no people. She said shortly, "The looms mistress will show you where you'll sleep. I'll be back to get you after you are clean. And remember this: Don't act so humble!"

"But I am humble!" I replied. "I'm nobody and I have nothing."

She stared at me. "Don't your parents love you? Didn't they grieve to see you go?"

Tears came to my eyes, and I nodded, unable to speak.

"Then they love you. And you say you have nothing! Act proud and you'll feel proud."

I curtsied acknowledgment.

Rhoda scolded: "Do you want the Lady Medea to pity you? She has enough troubles!"

So I had something to be proud about, and to honor the Princess I held my head high.

"Will you tell me about the other girls?" I asked.

"You'll find out soon enough."

"Do you come from far away?" I asked.

She looked at me with slitted eyes.

"I come from very far away," she said bitterly. "From the gates of death. Now don't ask any more stupid questions."

She walked out regally, with her head high.

Later I learned about Rhoda. Her parents would not come to her wedding. They didn't know she was alive. They had many children, and when she was born they did not keep her. According to custom, her father carried her out into the woods and left her on a mountainside to die. A shepherd found her, and a young couple without children brought her up. Rhoda was a brilliant girl with many skills and a golden future, but her hatred of her unknown, grieving parents spoiled her life.

The looms mistress bustled in. She was a woman about my mother's age, very worried looking — as she had a right to be, because she was in charge of all the Princess's companions. She was always in a hurry, always sighing, and always losing something, and her favorite expression was "I could scream!"

"You have a lot to learn," was the first thing she said. I started to cry, having heard that just once too often. She put her arm around me.

"Now, now, you *are* a country lamb, aren't you? Burst into tears when you're spoken to!"

"What do I have to learn? I was always a great help to

my mother. She taught me to spin when I was four years old."

"You probably had only coarse wool. You'll learn to spin fine thread from flax and do delicate weaving. You'll learn music and ritual dancing for ceremonial occasions. There's story telling — reciting poetry, that is — and the history of Colchis and the royal family. And manners, manners, manners.

"Each of the companions excels in something and teaches the others. Except Rhoda." She sniffed. "She excels in everything."

"I have nothing to teach anyone," I said wistfully.

"Never mind, the Princess wants you, and that's all that matters. Come with me to the common room. It's a large chamber where all the girls sleep."

She trotted down the corridor, while I tried to keep up. As we turned a corner, we saw an old woman sitting on a stone bench, bowed and grieving, with her mantle hiding her face but not all of her white hair. I stopped long enough to curtsy.

"Why did you do that?" the looms mistress demanded. "Did you think she is a great lady?"

"It is a custom we have at home," I explained. "We salute grief. It does not matter who the person is."

"It's a good custom," she agreed. "That poor old thing is always grieving. We call her Nurse. If she ever had a name, she lost it long ago. She is a very fierce old woman. She was the nurse of the older Princess, Chalciope, and of Medea and their younger brother, and also of the sons of Chalciope. She weeps for the sons. They sailed away on a journey of adventure, and nothing has been heard

19

from them. The fact is, nobody expects them back so soon, but Nurse is so sure they're dead that she has everyone else half convinced.

"She is very old now, and her sight is dim and her mind is no clearer than her eyes. She thinks of nothing but her little boys. They're grown men, but she forgets that.

"Sometimes she goes scolding through the palace, calling them, because she thinks they've run away."

"Where are the other girls?" I asked.

"In the meadow rehearsing a new dance. Rhoda is annoyed that she had to stay behind to greet you. Rhoda does everything better than anyone else, because she tries harder."

She pushed aside a tapestry hanging from a doorway. "Here is the common room. Your bed is over there. Keep your things in this chest—dear me, you didn't bring much, did you?"

She brought clothing out of the chest—a pink robe like the one Rhoda was wearing, and one of unbleached fabric, and one that was pure white wool.

"You have three dresses," she explained. "The girls will tell you each day what to wear." She glanced at me and laughed. "Your big eyes are almost out of your head, Country Lamb!"

"Three dresses," I gasped. "And all new! Oh, the Princess is so kind!"

"She certainly is. All her girls have clothes like these." She went to the doorway and called, and another woman brought a pitcher of hot water and a big bowl. "Take a bath, child," she suggested. "And wash your hair. Dear me, you're dusty. Put on the pink dress."

When I was bathed and clean, with the pink dress nicely draped, and my hair was in two neat braids, I didn't look like me any more. But I felt like me. Timid.

I resolved to do the very best I could, but I hoped it wouldn't be good enough for the fine people in the palace. Then they would send me home, and my mother would have to give back the donkey, but she wouldn't mind that. I could be more useful than a donkey any day.

Rhoda came in, light of foot and with her chin high, and said, "Sit down here, Daphne, while we talk. Each of us has some special talent, something we do very well and can teach to the other companions of the Princess. For instance, Doreen designs fine tapestry, and we all weave from her designs. Elsa is an artist — the paintings on the walls are hers. I play the lyre and the flute. Pelopia makes lovely jewelry, beating the gold with a tiny hammer. Hebe makes pottery, cups and plates and vases. The others you'll learn about as you meet them. And what can *you* teach us?"

I thought for a moment and answered sadly, "Nothing, my lady."

"But you must have some gift! Why else would she have asked to have brought you here?"

"Foresight and farsight — but only sometimes. And I don't think they can be taught."

"Ah, well, the Princess must have wanted you for that just the same. Remember, Daphne — always remember — everything we do is for the delight of Medea. When we have problems, she is not to know about them. We are here to make her glad.

21

"She is a girl like any girl, but she is also a princess and a priestess. So she is sometimes very lonely."

"What can I do for her, my lady?"

"Don't call me that!" she said crossly. "I am Rhoda. What you can do for her is — be kind. If she wants to be gay, you will learn how to amuse her. If she is melancholy, never approach her unless she invites you. And you must never be melancholy in her presence.

"If she is angry — and she can be very angry — if she should slap you or scream at you, never answer back." Rhoda smiled; it was almost a sneer. "Now you are afraid, aren't you?"

"Yes, I am." I shivered.

"Medea has burdens that you will never have. It is a fearful thing to stand between the people and the Dark Goddess. Medea must learn a thousand spells and charms, because she is a healer, too. She is often afraid, but she must never show it. Sometimes she must sacrifice a little pig or a lamb or a puppy — but she must always smile while she is at the altar. With blood dripping from her hands, she must smile and look glad to make the sacrifice."

"I will be kind to her," I promised in a whisper.

"During certain phases of the moon, Medea roams the mountains at night, alone, gathering herbs for her spells. She is in the mountains now. When she returns, she will be free for a while to enjoy herself with us, her chosen companions.

"It is a harsh service that she performs as priestess. She took it voluntarily two years ago from her older sister, Chalciope. She knew how hard it would be. But she accepted the burden because she loves her sister, who had carried it for so long."

"Today," I said, "coming into the city, I had a far-seeing. A young woman wearing black and weeping under a tree."

Rhoda's eyes widened. "She does wear black when she roams under the moon and when she goes to the altar in the poplar grove. You must be the only person who has ever seen the Lady Medea weep since she became a priestess. One of her obligations is that she must never cry in the sight of anyone.

"When she returns, she will perhaps want to talk with you. She will want us to dance for her in the meadow — she may lead some dances herself. And there is a game that we play — the dream game, we call it. She has the power to make us do strange things. Oh, don't worry about it — it's great fun. Her sister has the power, too. They can make us go to sleep and be almost anything. It's pleasant to be a cloud floating in the sky.

"You'll have lessons all day, getting ready for her return. We must teach you some of the dances. Do you play any musical instrument?"

"In festivals at home, I used to beat a little drum in the procession."

Rhoda sighed. "That must mean that you couldn't learn to do anything else. And I suppose you can't sing?"

"I try. But my tune is not the right tune."

"Oh, dear. After supper the King's harper will come and give us a history lesson about the royal family. He plays a lyre and sings poetry. We chant the choruses. Learn fast, Daphne. Everything we do is for Medea."

They taught me as fast as they could.

Weaving, of course, had to be done in the room where the looms were, but we spent much time out of doors in the private courtyard, spinning or embroidering or reciting our lessons. We memorized songs and poetry and had instruction in playing musical instruments. One of the longer songs was the history of the royal family, with every stanza ending, "The children of Helios have golden eyes."

It was a fact, the girls told me, that all the royal family, the king and his children, had eyes of so pale a brown that they were actually yellow.

It was hard for me to learn to sit still for lessons. At home I had a variety of tasks and responsibilities. But if the other girls had learned, so could I.

We could hear exciting things going on beyond the courtyard wall, but we couldn't see them. One day there was so much yelling and the sound of clashing weapons that I thought there was a battle going on.

Doreen laughed at me. "It's only a mock battle. The King's son, Apsyrtus, and his companions are having a test from their weapons master. If you think our education is hard, you should see what the Prince has to learn! Sometimes we climb up and watch — if the looms mistress isn't here to stop us.

"The Prince has to study government and justice and manners and music and ceremonials and religion and weapons and battle. I'd rather be me."

"*He* has to learn manners, too?"

"Nobody is born knowing," she answered. "And roy-

24

alty must not make mistakes that can be forgiven lesser people."

We learned the history of the royalty of Colchis.

The King had come from faraway Greece when he was a young man. He had inherited the kingdom of Corinth there, but he left a regent in charge and went wandering to the north and east, passing through many perilous adventures until he came to Colchis.

Chalciope and Medea were his daughters by his first wife. When Chalciope was of an age to marry, another wanderer came from Greece. His name was Phrixus, and he had to flee for his life from the city of Orchomenus, because an enemy there wanted to kill him.

Prince Phrixus married Chalciope, and they had four sons. He would have ruled in Colchis after the death of King Aeetes, through the inheritance of his wife, but he died. According to custom, his body was wrapped in oxhide and fastened on a branch of a big tree.

Some day another prince would come to marry Medea and rule in Colchis. She had had several suitors already, but she had not cared for any of them, and neither had King Aeetes.

Aeetes' son Apsyrtus was fourteen. When he grew up he would travel to far places to find a princess and a kingdom. (This was expected, but it was not fated, for he died young.) Chalciope's sons had recently sailed away for Greece to seek their brides and fortunes and to reclaim their father's kingdom of Orchomenus.

All this I learned, and every day — a dozen times a day — I had lessons in manners, manners, manners. Some

25

of the girls, especially Rhoda, made me feel that everything I did or said was awkward. Once when I felt that I'd never be able to please anyone, I started to cry. Doreen came over and sat down beside me. She put her hand on mine and murmured, "Daphne, don't blame the girls for admonishing you."

"I don't blame them," I sobbed. "I blame me for being stupid."

"You're not stupid at all. But some of the girls feel smart because they can tell you what to do. It's just the way people are. Some people. They build themselves up by tearing other people down. They don't mean to be unkind. They think about themselves so much that they can't think about others."

Then I felt sorry for them as well as for myself.

One day, running to get more wool for spinning, I took a wrong turn and came into a small, sunny courtyard that seemed more like home than anything else around the palace. Chickens were clucking and running around; they had nothing to eat, I noticed, and their water dish was empty. An old sow was grunting complaints in a corner with her brood of pigs around her.

So when I found my way back, after visiting the store room to get the wool, I told the looms mistress that I'd be glad to feed and water the chickens because they needed attention.

She looked shocked. "Leave the fowl alone," she warned. "They're kept for sacrifices, and only the royal family can attend to them. The Princesses are away, and the Prince apparently forgot. The King will have to take care of things."

She sailed out of the room to tell him.

I didn't see the King feeding the chickens, of course, but just thinking of it amused me. And thinking of the scolding he probably gave his son amused me, too. I had been scolded for carelessness like that myself, back home.

Many days had passed, and I had still not seen either princess. My education wasn't finished, although everybody was certainly working on it. One day I was running through the corridor to the common room, late for some reason, when I almost bumped into the old woman called Nurse. She was hobbling along by herself, scowling and muttering:

"Now where are those boys? I've looked all over, and it's time for their supper. Oh, I'll paddle them good, I will!"

She had a heap of cloth on one arm, narrow strips of wool that I recognized as the swaddling bands that small babies are wrapped in. Peering at me — the poor old lady saw movement, I suppose, but couldn't recognize faces — she demanded, "Have you seen the Lady Chalciope's babies?"

I bobbed a curtsy and answered politely that I had not.

Suddenly she dropped her bundle and cried out, "Oh, they're dead! They're dead! Fallen off the edge of the earth or swirling forever on the Ocean Stream or some monster's eaten them!"

"They are probably perfectly well," I told her. "Here, let me pick up those bands for you." She was groping for the things she had dropped.

27

I began to gather them, and suddenly I had a farseeing. It was very vivid.

"Why, they're alive!" I cried. "I see the young men —four of them—who wore these bands when they were babies!"

"They're dead!" Nurse insisted and pulled her mantle over her wrinkled face and wept. "Chalciope's four boys, all gone, and we'll never see them again!"

I couldn't promise that she would ever see them again, but I saw them at that moment very clearly.

"They are on the seashore," I told her. "Three are brown with the sun, and the fourth is sunburned and peeling; he has red hair and a fair skin. Their ship was wrecked—"

But she didn't care about their ship. She screamed so that my hair almost stood on end, and various people came running—including a couple of guards with swords in their hands and their helmets on crooked.

There was awful commotion. Someone grabbed me, and everybody yelled questions, and old Nurse kept shrieking, "Chalciope! Chalciope!"

A lady I had not seen before was suddenly there, a lady older than my mother but much younger than Nurse. She had golden eyes. She said a few words, firmly, and everyone quieted down except Nurse, who threw her arms around her and shouted:

"They're alive! She saw them! I don't know who she is, but she recognized Cytisorus by his red hair and sunburn. He always did peel instead of tanning."

3

―――――

"W<small>HO</small> <small>IS</small> this little girl?" the woman with golden eyes demanded.

Nurse cried, "What difference does that make? She says the boys are alive and well by the seashore somewhere. She is a farseer, and that's all that matters."

The woman put her arm soothingly around Nurse's bowed shoulders and spoke to me:

"I am Chalciope, and I thank you for news of my sons. What is your name?"

"I am Daphne, my lady." I remembered those lessons in manners and curtsied. "Sometimes I can foresee, but this was farseeing." I curtsied again. "I can tell, because I was touching something they had touched — your boys, I mean the Princes." Again I curtsied.

She smiled; she almost laughed. "Daphne," she said, "do stop bobbing up and down! We will go into my chamber, and you shall tell me just what you saw. Yes, Nurse, of course you may come with us."

I was calmer after we got away from all those excited people. A boy about fifteen came running into the chamber while I told the Princess about the farseeing, and she did not send him away. She asked me many questions, but I couldn't answer them, for the seeing had been only a glimpse.

She stood up and took my hand. "I want you to tell someone else," she said. "We'll go to the river. Apsyrtus," she said, turning to the boy, "where are the men working today?"

"I'll take you there," he offered. He had golden eyes, too. Realizing that this was the King's son, half-brother to Medea and Chalciope, I curtsied just to make sure he wouldn't feel slighted, but he didn't even notice. He was running toward the door, and we followed. The Princess was too dignified to run, but she walked so fast that I had to trot to keep up with her.

Down at the river bank, workmen were wading in the swift water, fastening sheepskins against a weir, and on

the bank several wet sheepskins were laid, glistening with specks of gold.

"Gold washes down in small grains," Apsyrtus remarked in a lordly way, "and this is how we get it out." He didn't look at me as he spoke, but he wasn't telling his sister anything she didn't know, so I bobbed another curtsy as a way of saying thank you. He had a perfect right to be condescending, of course, but I have noticed that big boys who aren't princes often speak that way to younger girls.

An old man with a gray beard, wearing a dark gray robe that was wet to the knees, turned from supervising the workmen. He looked surprised to see us there.

Chalciope pushed me forward, commanding, "Daphne, tell again what you saw."

With another curtsy, just to be on the safe side, I told the old man about the four young men, one of them sunburned and peeling.

He shouted, "Praise to Poseidon the sea god! He has saved my grandsons. Praise to the Dark Goddess and all the gods!"

His grandsons. He had bushy eyebrows, and he squinted in the sun so I couldn't see his eyes. But this was Aeetes, King of Colchis.

"Where is your sister?" he asked Chalciope.

"Still in the mountains, Father."

"There must be a gift for the little girl," the King said. "The first bracelet made from the gold we hauled in on the sheepskins today, that's what she is to have. Apsyrtus, tell the smith."

31

The Prince answered, "Yes, sir," and set off at a run.

A few days later Chalciope gave me the bracelet. I wear it yet and treasure it because it came from my home country.

"I'll be home as soon as I make sure the men put this treasure in a safe place," the King said. I curtsied. Chalciope laughed aloud this time and bent and kissed me. She took my hand, and we walked back toward the palace.

"You must be the little girl who saved the tax collector," she remarked. "And you were brought here because of the gifts you have. Now stop that bobbing, child. Nobody's watching.

"I never had that gift of yours," she said. "But my sister has it — and both of us have another one, in addition to the spells and rituals that I taught her when she trained for her obligations as priestess to the Three-Faced One. You will see my sister soon."

"But my lady, they said I still have so much to learn!" I cried.

"Nonsense. Learn it later," she advised. "Medea has been very busy since you came. First the moon was full, and she had long prayers to sing at Hecate's shrine. Now she is away, but when she returns her duties will not be taxing, and she will be free to enjoy her companions."

"I hope I'll do everything right, my lady," I sighed.

"Just be kind to her," Chalciope advised. "Amuse her. Entertain her. She's only eighteen years old. You'll all sing, and Medea with you. She plays the shepherd's flute very well, by the way. Do you play an instrument, Daphne?"

"They let me beat a little drum, my lady, but sometimes I do it at the wrong time."

"Don't worry about it," she advised. "Have you learned any dances yet?"

"I'm very bad in the dances," I confessed. "Yesterday we were doing one with ribbons, and I went the wrong way and we got all tangled up. Oh, my lady, I'm just not very good at anything — except spinning and weaving, and I can carry a heavy jar of water and I'm sharp-eyed at finding sticks for firewood and my mother trusted me to look after the younger children and keep the house neat."

Suddenly the tears came, as I remembered home. The Princess Chalciope murmured, "There, there, little Daphne," and knelt — think of it, she knelt beside me — and took me in her arms.

"We welcome you here," she said. "Never mind the things you haven't learned yet. Just remember that today your gift made all of us happy — and nobody else did that, only you!"

We walked on after she wiped my tears away with her robe's edge — of fine pale-gray wool, it was, with a narrow woven border of royal purple.

"My sister can farsee and foresee," she said, "but she could not see my sons, her nephews. You can farsee by touching a garment a person has worn?"

"Sometimes, my lady. And sometimes without touching, but not usually."

"Then I must warn you. Be very careful never to touch anything of my sister's when she is in the sacred grove. You might see her in the mysteries of worship, and you must not. Those are only for Hecate's priestess to know.

"I want to tell you about something else, Daphne. When you are with my sister something strange will happen to you, but it won't hurt and it won't frighten you. In fact, you won't even know it has happened until it's over. It is because of another power that my sister has. I have it too, but I don't use it any more. We call it the dream game."

I said politely, "Yes, my lady," and shivered.

4

THE NEWS SPED through the palace: "Medea has come home. She's sleeping now, but we'll see her tomorrow."

Doreen explained, "She was in the mountains, gathering herbs and saying spells. It has to be done at night." Doreen shivered. "I'd be afraid. Maybe she is, but it's part of the obligation."

"My mother gathered herbs for curing coughs and things like that," I remembered. "But in the daytime. She didn't say spells over them."

"Some of these cure wounds and sickness. Some are to burn for their sweet savor, and some," she lowered her voice to a whisper, "are deadly poison."

"What do they do with the poison ones?"

Doreen shrugged. "Nothing that I know of. It's just tradition and mustn't be forgotten. The princesses keep them in an ivory box, marked in special ways so they know which is which. Sometimes you'll see sick and injured people being brought in for healing. Maybe the princesses will even let you help — if you have a strong stomach and don't make a scene by fainting."

That night I had frightened dreams of doing everything wrong and being scolded by everyone and running but never getting anywhere. The girl named Hebe, whose bed was next to mine, was cross with me in the morning.

"You were a very noisy sleeper," she complained. "You kept crying out and waking me up."

"Nightmares," I said. "I'm sorry. You see, I'm afraid I'll do something wrong in the presence of the Princess."

"You probably will," Hebe said. Then she smiled. "But don't worry, Country Lamb. The Princess is not at all fearsome. We'll probably play games in the meadow, and maybe she'll want to lead a dance."

Hebe began to wash her face, and I thought of something new to worry about: "Oh, what shall we wear?" Then I realized how strange and wonderful it was to have any choice! For each of us had no less than three pretty robes — the pink ones and fine white linen ones that I hadn't yet seen anyone wearing and some of loosely woven wool, unbleached.

"The unbleached dress," Hebe advised. "Those are for play as well as work."

We were having our morning meal of fruit and bread and goat's milk in the common room — talking rather noisily, as a dozen girls usually do — when Rhoda's voice rose joyfully:

"My lady!"

We all stood, and for the first time I saw Medea. She was slim and small, with lovely fair hair in two long braids, and she really had golden eyes — so light a brown that they were yellow. She stood in the doorway, wearing an unbleached dress like all of us, and looked at us and smiled.

But she seemed strangely apart, almost dazed, because she was tired and had been afraid during her lonely wanderings in the mountains. I realized something important: This is what courage means, to be afraid but to go ahead because one's duty requires it.

There was a kind of spell over us. Medea brought awe into the room. She blinked, as if coming out of a spell herself, and came forward and said, "I am very glad to see all of you." Then she kissed Rhoda, and the golden eyes fell on me.

"The newcomer, Daphne," she said. "Welcome, Daphne." I curtsied, and she raised me up and kissed my cheek.

The other girls flocked around her, chattering and attentive.

"Shall we dance in the meadow?" she asked, and everyone answered, "Yes, yes!" One girl asked, "And may we play the dream game, my lady?"

Medea smiled. "Of course. It will be new to Daphne."

The meadow was lovely in the sun. Flowers were in bloom all through the grass. It seemed strange to wear sandals in the summer — at home we went barefoot except when there was snow.

We played games, counting out and chasing one another, and we ran races. Rhoda almost always won. Medea took part in some of the sports, but she seemed tired.

Then two smiling women servants appeared from somewhere, one with a shepherd's flute and the other with a lyre, so we had music for a simple circle dance — and I was lucky, for I didn't stumble once.

What, I wondered, was the strange thing that was going to happen that I mustn't be afraid of?

The Lady Medea sat down under a great shade tree, breathless from running and laughing. We sat around her. Two or three of the girls said eagerly, "The dream game?"

"What would you like to be?" she asked.

"Anything," someone said. Another girl suggested, "Clouds."

Doreen, sitting beside me, whispered, "You won't have any trouble. You'll just *be* a cloud."

The Princess took a little golden ball from a basket and held it up by its chain. The ball whirled, shining in the sun, as she rocked it. She was smiling as she spoke softly:

"It's warm and you're tired. Tired and sleepy. Sleep, sleep, Medea's maidens. Listen to the bees in the flowers."

Suddenly there was the sound of humming. It was a drowsy sound that Medea made. Some of the girls began to droop, with their eyes closed.

"It's all right to sleep, because you're tired, you've earned sleep, sleep, sleep."

She repeated those phrases, smiling, while the golden ball glinted in the sun. We were supposed to sleep, so I drooped, pretending.

"You are little clouds up in the summer sky," she murmured. "You're floating in the sky now, gently, gently."

All around me the girls rose to their feet and began to move gracefully about, with arms outstretched and faces upturned to the sun. It was very pretty, and I imitated

38

them to the best of my ability but with my eyes partly open.

"Now a storm is coming," Medea murmured. "The wind is rising, rising, rising. Little white clouds are storm clouds now, moving faster, faster."

The girls looked fierce, and some of them clenched their fists and struck the ground hard with their feet.

Medea watched us for a while, smiling. She said without raising her voice, "Daphne, come here." I approached her, feeling disgraced. "Sit down," she commanded. Then, to the others, "You're not clouds any more. You are little lambs, tired from playing. Rest now, lambs, sleep in the shade and rest."

The girls curled up on the ground and went happily to sleep.

Seated beside the Princess, I had a very clear seeing. It was so vivid that she wasn't there any more, nor were the meadow or the shade trees. When I saw her face again, she was looking at me intently.

"Sit down beside me, Daphne," she said. "You have the look of one who has seen something strange."

"My lady, you understand about the seeing. But I can't tell whether this is something happening now or something that will happen."

"I know," she answered. "What was it?"

"There was a ship on the sea, with many rowers in it. It is a magic ship — it can talk. I couldn't see that, but I know. One of the men is playing a lyre and singing in a great, sweet voice and another strikes hollow wood with wood to mark the beat of the oars for the rowers.

"They are brown from the sun, and their arms are strong, but I cannot tell whether they are slaves or kings. That was all, my lady — a talking ship that is the mother of these men. I don't know where they are."

Medea nodded. "I saw them yesterday. I do not think they are slaves."

"My lady, there were four faces that I could not see. I don't know any of the others, of course, but those four were hidden from me. The Princess Chalciope has four sons — "

"I think there will be a pleasant surprise for my sister," she agreed. For a moment she frowned. "I could see most of the faces, but there was one with a dark cloud obscuring it."

40

Medea said, "Each new girl who comes to be one of my companions receives a gift from my family. I haven't decided what yours shall be."

"I haven't done anything to deserve a gift, my lady. But if I may ask a favor — long ago, a man from my village became a hero. His name was Orthrus. He came here to the city to ask that food be sent to the starving people at home, and it was sent, but he died here."

"I know the story," she said. "The harper sometimes sings it. You would like to do honor to the hero?"

"Yes, my lady. And to kneel where his body is."

"I'll arrange it," she promised. "You didn't go to sleep at all when the other girls did," she said.

"I didn't go to sleep, my lady. I want to be obedient, but I couldn't go to sleep."

"The spell I put on the others doesn't work with you. I find that very interesting. You can't be hypnotized, like the others. Neither can I, although my sister has tried many times. Another day, I want to talk to you about your gifts. They can be a heavy burden." She sighed.

"My lady," I dared to tell her, "when the soldiers were bringing me into the city, I had a seeing of a fair-haired girl dressed all in black, leaning against a poplar tree. I think it was you. But she was not smiling. And the girls say you always smile."

She looked at me keenly. "Not always. But when sacrificing, I must always smile, although nobody mortal is there with me. At public ceremonies, of course, I must smile. It is not easy to remember to smile, so I do it often, because I must not forget.

41

"But sometimes when I am alone — my sister knows, because she was Hecate's priestess before me, but no one else knows or cares that I am sometimes afraid."

I shall never see her again, but I shall never forget the serene smile of Medea. That was the reason she was misunderstood after we left our own country and came here. How could any woman smile when she suffered? But Medea did.

It was little enough time that the Lady Medea had that day to be free with her maidens in the meadow. We were just starting another game when Rhoda said, "There is a man running toward us, waving his arms."

"A messenger," said Medea. "Something is wrong."

The man shouted, panting, "Some people are hurt, Lady. They need you."

She was instantly a different person, no longer a girl playing in the sunshine with other girls but a skilled wise woman with obligations. She veiled her face with part of her robe and moved swiftly toward the palace. She did not run; she glided. We who followed had to run to keep up.

"Two huts burned," the messenger panted, "and several people have been brought in for treatment. Your sister is with them."

Medea did not answer. She had been one of us. Now she was apart, alone, a woman of great dignity with knowledge that was not for us to understand.

A snake slithered through the weeds ahead of her, and she made a sign with her hand, for serpents belong to Hecate, but she did not hesitate. Nothing could delay the swift feet of Medea, concealed by her long robe.

She spoke just once, when we were close enough to hear the crying of the injured: "Rhoda, help me. Daphne, you may watch."

We could hear wailing and moaning. The other girls left us. Rhoda, I noticed, had her hands clenched into fists.

In the courtyard, Chalciope looked up from the screaming child she was attending and nodded to her sister.

Medea went at once to a man who lay on a litter, badly burned and moaning. Two women knelt beside him, crying.

One of them, his wife I suppose, kissed the hem of Medea's robe and sobbed, "My lady, he is so brave and good. He ran into the burning house and brought out three children."

"Go and comfort the children," Medea told her gently. She bent over the injured man. "I am Medea. I can ease your pain if you know I can. Do you hear me, brave man? Do you know me and believe?"

He moaned, "Yes, lady. I know you and believe."

"Sleep then," she said. "Sleep and rest. The pain is going away. It won't hurt very much now. Sleep, sleep, brave man. You have earned sleep."

He relaxed and was quiet, but he was not asleep, although he was more comfortable.

"The herbs for burns," Medea said, not turning from him.

Then I saw that Rhoda was sick from the sight of all this. She was very white and was swaying where she stood. She sat down, helpless, on the ground.

There were some jars on a bench with dried leaves in

43

them. I sniffed and recognized some of them by the odor as the very same my mother used for burns. I beckoned to one of the servants who had just come with a bronze bowl of steaming water. I put some of the leaves into a shallow dish and she poured hot water on them.

Then I moved the dish back and forth, blowing on the mixture to hasten the cooling. I held out the dish to Medea, who was chanting a magic spell of which I couldn't understand a word. When the wet leaves had cooled, she laid them gently on the man's burned skin.

His wife implored, sobbing, "Will he live, my lady?"

Smiling, Medea answered, "It is in the laps of the gods, as all of us are. He will be scarred, but I think he will live."

Seeing her smile, over a burned and suffering man, I shivered. But the smile was part of her obligation.

A few days later, the looms mistress announced, "This morning Daphne will receive her gift from the Lady Medea. All of you are to take part in the ceremony. It will be in the cemetery grove."

There was a gasp among the girls, and the looms mistress snapped, "Stop that whispering! Loosen your braids. For this ceremony you'll go with your hair unbound. And take off your bracelets."

We walked across the great meadow, chanting a mourning song and carrying bundles of dried rushes to burn. A dozen spearmen marched beside us, not for protection but as an honor guard, and an old man, the Priest of All Gods, walked ahead. Next after him was the King's bard with his lyre, and after him walked Medea. Behind her maidens came two men beating drums slowly as for a funeral.

I was frightened, and some of the other girls were pale. The cemetery grove was a dark, dank place of great trees that shut out the sun, and in the trees were big bundles that were the honored dead of Colchis. Dead men, only men. We buried the bodies of women and of proved cowards, but brave men were wrapped in oxhides and tied on tree branches.

The wind was blowing, making a roaring and a rattling on the stiff oxhide bundles. Under one tree the procession stopped and Medea bowed three times. That was to the honor of Chalciope's husband, Prince Phrixus. Then we went on.

Under another tree Medea herself laid the dried rushes on a low altar of earth, and a servant handed her a torch and she lighted the fire. All in silence, except for the booming and rattling of the wind and the thudding of the funeral drums, she gave me grain to burn, and I scattered it on the fire in honor of Orthrus, the hero from our village.

Then the Lady Medea sang a chant of praise for him, and I poured a libation of wine on the fire.

Later she instructed the tax collector to tell the people back home, on his next visit, that these things had been done by order of the King's daughter, and that this was her gift to Daphne in honor of a village from which so brave a man had come.

5

When the Princess moved with stately grace and smiled as if remembering joy, then she was sore afraid. When terror froze her heart, she could never admit it. Hecate's priestess was not permitted to show by any sign that fear or horror touched her.

The first public ceremony after I went to the King's city was a religious festival honoring Hecate, the three-faced moon. It was held in the market square. There was a solemn procession with chanting and the waving of leafy branches. To the altar, Medea carried a squealing little pig.

She cradled it in her arms and crooned a lullaby, and she smiled as she plunged the bronze knife into its throat.

A great moan of relief went up from the people, for this sacrifice protected us from the anger of the Dark Goddess. They rushed forward to dip leaves and bits of cloth into the blood.

Medea held her dripping hands over the altar and smiled for the awesome goddess.

It is no wonder that people outside her homeland could never understand my lady Medea. She could not react in time of terror as ordinary mortals do. She had been trained to conceal what she felt.

46

And so, later, when she had enemies, they said she never felt anything at all. They made her seem a monster.

The greatest festival of the year took place in midsummer. This was the Mystery of Life Renewed, symbolic of the promise that although we must die, each of us will be born again.

It was carried out in every community in Colchis, and even beyond the borders, but in the city I saw it for the first time in all its awesome splendor.

Medea and her sister officiated, but everyone took part.

The festival came on the night when the thin new moon rose over the forest.

Two days earlier there were processions with banners and mourning music, with wailing chants of grief for the death of the moon, which is Hecate. We were in mourning until the new moon dawned. Then all the people dressed in their best clothes and went by torchlight to the Field of Ares to watch an aged ram become a young, skipping lamb.

There was steady, monotonous drumming, and in a great tree a shield, shining in the firelight, twisted and turned. All the people stared at it and waited.

The two priestesses led a feeble, limping old ram to the middle of the field while the people watched in awed silence. But when the sisters put the old ram into an immense caldron, everyone chanted — and when a little, dancing lamb leaped out, we shouted with joy. The thin new moon came into sight. After that, there were games and mock battles and ritual dances and a feast.

The old died, the new was born again. That was the promise, that death is not forever.

On the morning of the worst day that ever dawned for Colchis, there was fog on the River Phasis, fog that even swirled in the palace courtyards. There is a song now about that day. The song tells that the fog was sent by the gods to conceal the men who had beached their ship in the marsh and were approaching the palace — the men from a ship called *Argo*.

We who attended Medea were afraid of her that morning. She said briefly that she had dreamed something awful was going to happen. She was restless, broke a thread in her weaving, and paced in the weaving room, not caring to talk. We worked silently at our various tasks, but one thing after another went wrong. Someone dropped a shuttle. Someone else dropped a clay cup that shattered on the floor.

Medea frowned, picked up her lyre and ran her fingers over it — and a string snapped. She threw down the lyre and the tortoise shell back cracked. Angrily, she walked out of the room.

The looms mistress noticed that the Princess had left the tiny basket in which she kept her golden ball. But two girls refused to take it to her — she had slapped one of them and scolded the other. Medea always carried the golden ball, sometimes wearing it on its chain as a necklace, sometimes tying the tiny basket to the girdle of her robe.

"Daphne," the looms mistress whispered, "follow her. Take this."

I could not refuse. I ran after the Princess — and heard her scream with pure fright. In the courtyard she stood staring at a group of seven young men. They were like spirits in the swirling fog.

Medea's maidens streamed out to see what was the matter, and from another door Chalciope and her ladies came running.

Chalciope cried, "My sons! My boys!" and four of the young men ran toward her with their arms outstretched. Poor old Nurse came hobbling, and they embraced her, too.

At that moment the sun broke through the fog and shone on the golden hair of Medea. She stood transfixed, staring. A rosy flush came and went in her smooth cheeks.

The tale we hear now is that the little god of love shot her in the heart with an unseen arrow when she looked for the first time on the face of Jason. Ill-fated Medea · — that moment changed her life. I stood beside her and offered her the basket, but she pushed it away.

The courtyard swarmed with people, the King among them. He embraced his grandsons. One of them spoke formally for all:

"Grandfather, we were shipwrecked in a storm and cast ashore. These three foreigners — they are all kings or princes — and others in their ship rescued us.

"This man, their leader, is named Jason. He is under an obligation. He asks your help."

Chalciope's son swallowed as if he did not want to go on.

"He must take back to Greece the golden fleece of the great ram on which our father, Phrixus, rode when he came here to Colchis long ago. Jason's country suffers from plague and drought, and an oracle said he must bring back the fleece and give the body of our father proper burial."

King Aeetes replied briefly: "I thank the foreigners for saving my grandsons, but the rest of that is nonsense, as you well know."

Chalciope said piteously, "Let us discuss this quietly before you make your decision. They did rescue your grandsons!"

The King made a gesture, and his guards began to move the crowd out of the courtyard.

How I wished to be somewhere else! But Medea would

not take the basket — she seemed to be in a trance. I had to stay beside her.

When the crowd had moved out, Argeus spoke again: "Jason is a relative of ours, Grandfather. Our father's father was his grandfather's brother. And these visitors have promised, in return for your help, to conquer your enemies, the children of the Amazons."

"Arrogance, pure arrogance," the King growled. "I'll take care of my own enemies — including the Greeks! They've come to conquer Colchis!"

Chalciope plucked at his sleeve and calmed him a little. She whispered to him urgently and at length. He turned to the young man and said:

"The foreigners are our guests, although uninvited. You say they are kings and princes in their own countries, so we will entertain them properly during the very short time they stay here.

"Make ready a feast!" He gestured, and the servants began to run out. "Prepare baths and give them wine!" The courtyard emptied fast.

Then he turned and scowled at his younger daughter. Medea turned, blushing, and absently accepted the little basket from my hand. I followed her into the palace. She walked silently into her own chamber.

There was an explosion of activity in the weaving room. The girls clustered around, asking me a hundred questions. The looms mistress shouted, "Be quiet! Oh, I think I'll scream!" A woman servant ducked in with a message:

"There will be a formal presentation of the guests after the banquet, Lady Chalciope says. And guess how many of them there are! Almost fifty! The rest were back with the ship in the marsh."

You can't keep anything quiet in a palace — the servants observe, unnoticed, and spread the news.

"I heard there is even a girl with them, but nobody knows for sure," she added as she slipped out.

Rhoda spoke: "There was a presentation ceremony when I first came here. I remember it. We'll accompany Medea into the throne room after the banquet. We must rehearse the procession."

Chalciope came in then, looking harried. With her was a tall young woman wearing a short robe, quite dirty, and with her dark, snarled hair bundled up in a coarse net. She was deeply tanned, and she carried a bow in her hand and a quiver of arrows on her shoulder. She stared at us all as if she wouldn't object to some kind of argument, and we stared back.

Chalciope spoke to the girl: "Lady Atalanta, these are the maidens of my sister Medea. Bring my sister here, one of you." Rhoda ran out to get her. "The Lady Atalanta will have a chamber to herself."

Medea entered, gliding. In the few minutes since her father sent her from the courtyard she had transformed herself. She wore a white robe with a border of royal purple, and her hair was beautifully arranged. She was a princess indeed.

Chalciope introduced them: "My sister, Princess Medea, priestess of the goddess of Hecate. The maiden Atalanta, from Arcady, vowed to the goddess Artemis."

We had heard of Artemis, the virgin huntress, but she

52

was not worshipped in Colchis except as one of the three phases of Hecate: maiden, mother, and crone.

Medea and Atalanta bowed to each other.

Chalciope explained, "In the presentation, Lady Atalanta will walk behind me and sit beside me at the King's left. When the flutes begin a new melody, sister, six of your girls will go in, by couples, then you, then the other six.

"You girls will remain standing until Princess Medea is seated. Then you sink to the floor around her chair — gracefully, like doves settling. Rhoda, you will teach them. The feast won't be ready until sunset. Now, Atalanta — " She swept out, burdened with many cares. The tall huntress followed with long strides.

I murmured to Elsa, "At home, we would find out who these strangers are before we welcome them."

"That's not how kings do it, Country Lamb," she answered. "For a king to question noble guests before they're fed would be bad manners. He knows they're important. After the feast, they'll all be named."

Rhoda ordered, "Come into the antechamber of the throne room. We'll rehearse there."

The courtyard was a bustle of activity. Some of the King's men had slaughtered a big bull and were butchering it. Others were running with wood for the fires. Women trotted along carrying big water jars.

I said to one of the girls, "I'm only a country lamb, but this I do know: The meat of that old bull is going to be very tough."

She answered, "I think the King is going to honor these

53

strangers just as much as he has to and not one bit more. If their teeth aren't strong enough for the meat, how can they complain?"

We passed by a big room full of big men — and let me tell you, we stared. They were taking off their armor, piece by piece, so that the servants could clean it up. The four grandsons of the King were pouring wine for them. It was not the best wine — we could tell by the marks on the jars.

Rhoda showed us how to sink like doves settling. We walked into the empty throne room, to the music of a flute, and sank around an empty chair — but not very much like doves.

"You are crows!" Rhoda scolded. "Chattering like crows and just as graceful! Once more — eyes down, hands softly folded, walk slowly but don't drag your feet — and don't chatter. When you are in place, sink down, like this."

She demonstrated, and I did want to be a dove instead of a crow.

"If one of you is awkward," she warned, "all those highborn heroes from far away will laugh long after they get home. They will tell their grandchildren about the crows of Colchis. Now once more. You are doves — but don't flutter and don't coo!"

We practiced until she was satisfied — and our leg muscles began to hurt. It's not easy to sink like a dove. But once you get the idea, it's pleasanter than gleaning in a grain field or picking up olives under a tree or beating clothing with a paddle in cold spring water when the family wash has to be done.

The King's servants scurried around, and Medea's maidens would have done the same thing except that the looms mistress kept reminding us sternly to be dignified.

In spite of all the hurry and confusion, the servants found moments to dart in and tell us what they had found out about the foreign visitors. Servants find out a great deal — some of it not true at all.

The looms mistress was frantic, between wanting to hear everything and reminding us that we shouldn't believe a word of it.

One of the girls giggled and whispered, "I know for a fact that she promised two of the serving women new mantles if they would keep bringing news. Of course *we'll* weave the mantles!"

The dangers the foreign lords had overcome were fantastic, according to the tales we heard.

Some of them were descendants of gods, the servants told us, awe-struck. Orpheus was the name of one man; he was a sweet singer, and his mother was one of the Muses. Another was Melampus, a prophet; his father was the sea-god Poseidon.

The servant said, "Melampus can understand the speech of birds! He got that power from a brood of young serpents — he saved them from death, and they licked his ears so that he can hear things unknown to other men. And he prophesies by examining the insides of sacrificed animals."

The looms mistress looked shocked and said, "How nasty!"

"I'm only telling you what they said," the servant insisted. "And he's not the only one. The man named

Mopsus can foretell the future by watching the movements of drops of olive oil on the surface of a basin of water and can do something by shaking a quiver of arrows and studying the arrow that falls out first."

"Let us hear no more of that," the looms mistress ordered. "When the gods want us to know what is going to happen, they show us. But to force them to tell us, with these magic methods — why, that is irreverent, and no good will come of it!"

The servant replied sullenly, "I can't help it if these foreigners do what they shouldn't do. I'm only telling you what I heard." She turned to leave the room but added over her shoulder, "Furthermore, the ship they came in has something magic about it. Sometimes it talks!" She flounced out.

The looms mistress clapped her hands for attention and ordered, "Girls, pick up all the threads and scraps in this room at once — and don't tell the Princess a word of this nonsense about the foreigners being able to prophesy the future. Maybe they can, but they shouldn't."

No women were present at the feast. That was not customary in Colchis. We ate in our common room — and the meat *was* tough.

There were a thousand things we wanted to know about the sunbronzed strangers, whom we had only glimpsed, but we didn't dare, although one of them ate with us — the girl Atalanta.

Now that she was cleaned up, she looked better than I expected. Her curly dark hair had been dressed in a neat knot at the back, with a few curls around her face, and she wore a white robe that covered up those long, tanned legs.

She was a strange girl indeed. She didn't care whether we liked her, and we *didn't* like her. She boasted. Now that I am older, I can understand that she needed us for an audience to impress with her boasting, because she had been deprived of so much that every girl has a right to expect.

"I came all the way with the Argonauts," she told us, "and I can pull an oar with any of them — except Heracles, of course, the strong man. But we left him behind by accident several weeks ago.

"They didn't invite me to come along — no, they certainly did not! But I was looking for adventure, so I stowed away — and that's not easy. I didn't announce myself until *Argo* was hours out from port. They had made the proper sacrifices, prayed for a good wind and got it, and they couldn't turn back then."

She laughed, "Haw haw!" remembering.

"As an archer, few of them can beat me. We lived off the country, of course, hunting wild game wherever we pulled up the ship and camped. We had some battles with the natives in some places. I can't cast a spear as far as some of the men, but my arrows tasted blood."

What could we say to that? Nothing. We just stared at her. Poor Atalanta. Everything she did all her life was awkward. She didn't fit anywhere.

She looked around the table at us and remarked, "I suppose you were all given to the Princess by your parents because they didn't want you at home?"

We cried out, "No, no, my lady!" — except for Rhoda, who glared at her.

"My father didn't want me," Atalanta said gruffly. "He wanted a boy baby, so he had a serving woman put me up in the mountains — and here I am." She shrugged as if it didn't matter, but of course it did matter terribly.

I was proud to remember that my father was too kind to cast out even the youngest children in our family.

"But I'll show him," Atalanta promised, scowling. "I know now who he is. And he knows who I am! I am Atalanta — they call me Mistress of the Straight-Shot Arrow. They call me the Fleet Runner. I've beaten every one of the Argonauts in foot races."

She picked up a chunk of meat in both hands and talked around it.

"I'll go to see my father when we get back — if we get back. Then let's see if he won't be proud to claim me, even if I am a daughter instead of a son!"

When the time came for the ceremony, six of us walked ahead of Medea and six behind her, to the music of flutes — not fluttering very much.

She was a vision, my princess. The goddess Aphrodite must be more beautiful, but I think no mortal woman could be. Medea's long blonde hair hung in curls brought forward over her shoulders, and she was decked with ornaments made of white metal. It is not silver, not gold, but a cunning mixture of the two.

A fragile diadem with tiny metal leaves was in her hair, and she wore matching necklaces and bracelets, with all those tiny leaves shimmering on fine chains. Her gown was soft linen, not quite white, but silvery.

58

She walked with her eyes down, pale as the moon. When the guests saw her, there was a great sigh of admiration.

I know now that she was a girl in love and that her heart was beating like a bird trying to get out of its cage.

While she was taking her seat, we stood, fluttering just a little at sight of the guests, the strong heroes from distant lands. Then we sank like doves settling, and all the practice was worthwhile.

They were sunbrowned and muscular, dark-skinned against the white of their court garments. They wore scars from their battles. Their hands were calloused from pulling the oars of their ship, and all of them had squint wrinkles from the sunlight on sea water.

Even when none of them moved, there was a strangeness in the room because there were so many of them and they were so bold and strong. The room was full of leashed power.

They were tense and watchful, wary but not afraid.

The presentation began. Men servants brought each guest his polished shield. The King sat in his chair of state with the armed men of his guard behind him.

Chalciope's son Phrontis was the official crier. He carried a herald's staff with white ribbons twined around it. He stood facing his grandfather and lifted the staff and chanted, "My lord, this is Admetus, lord of Pherae, rich in sheep."

One of the Argonauts marched up to the King's chair holding his shield on his left arm for identification and laid his sword across the King's knees.

The King handed back the sword and said, "Admetus,

lord of Pherae, deserving of honor," and the drums sounded.

Prince Phrontis proclaimed, "Coronus, son of valorous Caeneus, from Gyrlon," and another man marched up. Again the King gave back the sword and acknowledged, "Coronus, son of valorous Caeneus, deserving of honor," and the drums rolled.

And so they came, one by one or two by two if they were brothers:

"The sons of Aeacus, Telemon from island Salamis, and Peleus, lord of Phthia.

"Polydeuces and Castor from Sparta, strong in battle.

"Meleager, son of Oeneus of Calydon." He was only a boy.

The huntress Atalanta leaned forward, yearning. For all her tomboy ways, she was in love with Meleager.

"Zetes and Calais from goodly Thrace, sons of the North Wind." Big men, those, and they wore strange sandals with bronze wings on the back.

"Mopsus the strong seer, skilled in augury with birds.

"Jason, son of Aeson, rightful heir to the throne of Iolcus."

This time Medea yearned forward, and the color in her cheeks changed from white to red and back again. King Aeetes seemed to hesitate about handing this man back his sword. Jason was the leader of the whole expedition.

Then the herald intoned, "Orpheus the sweet singer, lord of Pieria," and I was swept with sudden knowledge of this smiling man. In him was goodness wedded to strength, and with these was courage beyond measure.

60

Ah, Orpheus! I was very young, but first love is nothing to laugh at. Fortunate the maiden whose first love is worthy! It is well if she can be proud of the one for whom her heart first beat faster.

Later, Orpheus was kind to me — but he was kind and courteous to everyone. I grieve for Orpheus, as do all who ever knew him. He is dead in Thrace, but there is a constellation in the sky that we call the Lyre of Orpheus. Sometimes on the rooftop I look up at those stars and know that his shade walks with the heroes in the asphodel of the Elysian Fields. Those who dwell there are cheered by his music.

Prince Phrontis continued with the presentation, but I did not hear a single name after that of Orpheus. My eyes sought him out among the sunbrowned, hard-muscled companions. Orpheus the sweet singer, deserving of honor.

The presentation took a very long time, of course. Phrontis, acting as herald, then announced:

"Now the Lord Jason wishes to tell the King the reason for this journey."

Aeetes bowed his head regally and replied, "The King will hear the Lord Jason."

Jason began to talk.

"My lord, I am the son of Aeson. My Uncle Pelias wrongfully rules the land of Iolcus and keeps my father imprisoned in the palace. I was brought up in the mountains. I returned to Iolcus to claim the kingdom, and Pelias promised it to me if I would free the land of a curse. He is haunted by the ghost of the great Phrixus, who was the husband of your daughter Chalciope.

61

"Pelias said that Phrixus had fled here to your kingdom long ago, to avoid being sacrificed. He came riding on a great ram with a golden fleece. Pelias said that Phrixus haunts him because he was denied proper burial."

Aeetes stiffened and began to tap his hand on the arm of his throne. He replied: "Phrixus had the honors of a great prince at his funeral. Pelias lied."

Jason said quite meekly, "Yes, my lord, he is a liar. But he told me I must bring back the golden fleece and the spirit of Phrixus, your son-in-law. I know the fleece hangs from a tree and is guarded by an unsleeping dragon."

There was a stir among the people in the room, because this was pure nonsense. Golden fleece? The river was full of them. Dragon, indeed! One of the girls in our group began a giggle but changed it into a cough.

Jason continued: "So I sent messengers to these lords who are here before you and gathered them together. Argus the Thespian built us a fine ship, for fifty rowers, and the goddess Athena herself fitted a beam into the prow made from the magic oak at Dodona. The ship is the *Argo*, and the oaken beam sometimes speaks to us.

"Our journey has been long and dangerous, my lord. Some of us who started in Argo are now dead on foreign shores, and some were left behind by accident.

"The great Heracles, the strongest man in the world, is not with us any more. When his young servant Hylas was drowned in a spring, Heracles went mad with grief, and we sailed away, not knowing that he was raging through the woods. Idmon the prophet was killed by a wild boar in a swamp. Tiphys the helmsman is dead."

The King mumbled politely, "I share your grief." He yawned, being tired and old. He wasn't the only one who got sleepy as Jason continued. Two of the Lady Medea's maidens dozed, but we who sat behind them kept nudging them awake. Jason told one story after another of the Argonauts' adventures. The Lady Medea hung on every word. King Aeetes rose from his throne, and the young heroes stood up to hear his decision. He spoke sarcastically. Golden flames seemed to shoot from his eyes.

"You'll have to earn what you came to get," he said. "Lord Jason is your leader, so he will perform the tasks I'm going to set."

I heard Medea draw in a sharp breath.

"You may take the magic golden fleece if you dare, but first you must find it. And before you can look for it, you must work for it.

"No doubt you saw the bronze-footed bulls at my gate. On the Plain of Ares you must find two like them; they breathe flames. Harness them, and plough the plain."

The girl beside me seized my hand and squeezed it. We knew there were no such live bulls. How could anyone plough with them?

"Then plant some seed that we keep here — the teeth of a great serpent that once persecuted the city of Thebes. Armed men will grow up out of the ground. You must kill them all with your spear.

"Day after tomorrow you will do this — and finish it before nightfall. Then you may try to take the golden fleece."

He turned toward the door and started out so briskly

that his spear guards stumbled in catching up with him. The King of Colchis was a tired old man — and very, very angry.

He was trapped, by his own grandsons and the laws of royal hospitality, in a situation that looked disastrous for his people.

6

THE ROYAL FAMILY filed out of the throne room with
their attendants — all but Medea. She leaned forward in
her chair and gazed across the room at Jason. Then, realizing that the ceremony was finished, she blushed and
arose, and we followed her out.

One of the girls whispered to me, "We go with her into
her chamber, and then she dismisses us. She may want
one or two of us to help put away her jewelry."

Medea didn't seem to know or care that we were with
her. She entered her chamber, picked up a hand mirror
of polished bronze, and stared at her reflection as if she
had never seen it before. We hovered in the background,
not making a sound.

Then, as if asleep, she began to remove her bracelets,
and because I happened to be nearest she put them into
my hands. Out of the corner of my eye I saw the rest of
the girls tiptoe out. And from down the corridor I heard
the King's angry voice coming closer, and Chalciope's
voice trying to soothe him.

The King swept into the room, and I couldn't get out
without being conspicuous, so I pretended not to be
there. Nobody noticed me.

Chalciope kept touching his arm to get his attention. She said, "Father." She said, "My lord." She said, "King Aeetes!" He paid no attention to these interruptions but went on scolding:

"I'll show them a thing or two. Coming here with all that nonsense — do they think I'm a half-wit who would believe it? I don't doubt they had some dangerous experiences — that's reasonable, the distance is great, and there were enemies to oppose them. But if they think I'll believe all those lies! Chalciope, you know better. Your own husband, Phrixus — you know he didn't come here riding any golden ram!"

Chalciope murmured, "Yes, Father, I know he didn't. He never said he did. He came in a ship with a gilded ram's head on the prow."

"Then where do they get that foolish story? And why do they expect me to believe it? Do they think I don't know anything about the world outside my own kingdom? Do they think I was born in Colchis?"

"We know you weren't born here," Chalciope said soothingly. "We know you came from Corinth. You made just as long and dangerous a journey as they did."

"A longer journey!" the King roared. "Corinth is far to the south of the port their ship sailed from. And more dangerous! Because *I* came part of the way overland, and my men and I fought some bitter battles on the way, let me tell you!"

"Yes, Father," his older daughter agreed. "We know you did. And tomorrow you can tell them. But you really should go to bed now and get your rest. It's very late."

66

That only set him off again. "Tell them? I could tell them, but of course they'd never believe it. Oh, no. They know everything, those fellows do. They know all about a golden fleece from a magic ram, and they say it's here, and you may be sure they won't sail off until they get it.

"There is no such thing, I can tell them, but will they answer, 'Yes, Aeetes, we believe you'? Of course not. They'll think I'm lying, and there'll be a fight. My soldiers can whip that lot — less than fifty of them — I don't care how royal they are, my men can kill every one of them. But we'd have wailing widows in Colchis if it came to a battle, and I've got to avoid that."

Medea spoke for the first time. "Lord King," she said gently, "may I consult with my sister Chalciope about a plan that has come to me? Do you trust your daughters?"

The old King stared at her as if he had forgotten she was there.

"I'm not sure I trust either of you!" he roared. "Chalciope admires these Argonauts because they rescued her sons. And you, young lady, don't think I wasn't watching the way you looked at Jason during the ceremony!"

Medea covered her blushing face with her mantle.

Chalciope said gently, "Father, do let me talk to my sister about her plan, whatever it is. Nothing needs to be decided tonight. Now you need rest. Let me prepare a potion that will help you sleep."

"Talk about it right now," Aeetes commanded.

"The dream game," Medea said softly. "Both Chalciope and I can cast the spell. It doesn't need to be just

67

a game for my girls in the meadow. You know we use it in treating the sick. It lessens pain, because the sick person believes it will."

"These intruders aren't sick, they're mad," the King argued.

"You can't afford to anger them, Father. If Jason *thinks* he does those brave deeds — if the audience sees him do them — what more is needed?"

The King looked startled. "Can you control the audience of strangers?"

"We hypnotize everyone who comes to the Mystery of Life Renewed. They know something strange will happen to them."

"But the strangers — the foreigners?"

"Let them know. Make them believe — and let them be fearful of unknown wonders. The only person I've met who can't be made to dream is that little girl from upcountry."

Chalciope suggested, "There is tomorrow to spread the word to the foreigners, to make them afraid. The servants will do it — especially if they're told not to."

The King said thoughtfully, "It's the only hope to avoid a battle. If some of the foreigners *don't* see Jason plough with the bulls and kill the Sown Men and overcome the dragon, they won't want to admit it for fear of making him look like a fool. But what if your spell doesn't delude Jason himself?"

"Then everything is lost," Medea answered. "I only want to save his life!"

The morning after the presentation of the noble guests,

Medea's maidens were a bunch of crosspatches. All of us had been up late. Three or four of us woke up very early, because the ceremony had left us tense and excited. We tried to tiptoe around, but we disturbed the other girls who wanted to sleep. That made them cross, and most of us said some things we were sorry for.

One girl slapped another one, and both of them burst into tears. At that moment, Princess Chalciope swept into our sleeping chamber.

"Shame on you!" she said. "Not dressed, not washed, your hair uncombed — and I could hear you far down the corridor! My sister requires you to attend her. As doves, not crows."

We murmured respectfully, "Yes, my lady," and tried to look like doves.

"The visiting lords were up and out long ago. They will put on an exhibition of war skills and races of some kind. Medea will honor them by leading you in several dances. The King will be there. Wear your pink dresses — and hurry!"

She swept out again, and there was a great rush for combs and water jugs. We had two small burnished bronze hand mirrors for the twelve of us; they are very costly. Several small arguments broke out — in whispers — about taking turns with the mirrors, because we all wanted to look our best.

Serving women brought in our fruit and bread, but none of us ate very much. We looked neat and respectable as we trooped to Medea's room. She looked beautiful but worried.

69

She addressed us: "We shall go to the meadow to dance. It is proper that we should entertain my father's guests. They will also entertain my father and his court. There is some thought that these visitors may be — dangerous."

Medea stopped and looked with pleading at her sister. Chalciope then spoke:

"They are trained in warfare, while in Colchis we are a peaceful people. These foreign kings and lords might attack if they become angry. The King has strong soldiers, but of course he does not want any fighting."

She nodded to Medea to continue. Medea spoke as if she had memorized the speech against her will:

"The King owes an obligation to the guests, both because they are his guests and because they rescued his grandsons. But the men of the ship *Argo* have demanded something that the King cannot give them because there is no such thing — a magic golden fleece from a ram that they say came here carrying Phrixus on its back. There is no use telling them this story is nonsense, because they are sure it is true, and they will only think we're lying to make it hard for them to get the golden fleece."

Medea swallowed, as if speaking were difficult. "And so we shall entertain them in the meadow, we shall be courteous — and we shall try to find a way to satisfy the Argonauts and get them out of our country with no harm done to anyone."

What a buzzing there was among Medea's pink doves as we walked out to the meadow! We were accompanied by a guard of twelve spears, and we couldn't help glancing up at their shining body armor and admiring their stern faces under the helmets. One girl started to whimper:

70

"Are the Argonauts going to kill us?"

"Nonsense!" laughed the captain of the guard. "We're here just to prove that King Aeetes has so many soldiers that he can even spare some to chase off butterflies if they bother you girls."

We whispered among ourselves: "Medea's in love with the yellow-haired one, Jason . . . Who wouldn't be? Ah, to be a king's daughter! . . . I like the twins, with the metal wings on their sandals . . . What's the name of the one who sings so well? . . . Ask Country Lamb — she's in love with him. Look at her blush! . . . No use losing your heart to any of them — they'll sail away soon, and we'll never see them again."

The guard captain muttered, "I wouldn't have believed it, but that girl who came with them is out there with armor and arms!"

One of the spearmen laughed and asked, "If she comes at me with a spear, how polite do I have to be?"

Sure enough, the tall Atalanta was with the young lords, practicing at spear-casting.

The captain said, with admiration, "Look at her run! She's fast on her feet, that one. Her spear barely touches the ground before she's caught up with it."

That was a lovely day in the meadow. The King and his Queen and their attendants sat in the shade of a great tree. Apsyrtus was with them, and so were Chalciope's four sons.

Medea and Chalciope sat under another tree, where robes had been spread. We settled like doves, and the spearmen stood around us, their armor rattling a little when they changed position.

71

The Argonauts finished their spear-casting, and Jason held up his arm in a salute to the King. Then they put on an exhibition of fighting with short swords and shields. It was very noisy, as the metal blades clashed against the metal or hard bull's hide of the shields. The whole thing was like a ceremonial dance, with two of the men beating time on big, booming drums. Nobody got hurt, but Medea's maidens were breathless when it was over, because we thought there would be bloodshed. I never took my eyes off Orpheus the sweet singer. He was as skilled with arms as he was with music.

The visiting lords finally handed their swords and spears over to some of the King's servants and unbuckled their armor. Then, laughing and sweating, they strolled over to the tree where the King sat, saluted properly, and sat on the ground. Servants brought them towels and cups of wine and water for refreshment.

Chalciope said in a low voice, "Now!"

Medea instructed us: "First, Birds Flying. Then the Rescue of Andromeda. Then we rest a little. After that, the Nereids in the Sea, and finish with the ribbon dance."

That was the hardest, and she must have heard me sigh. "Daphne, come back here and sit down before the ribbon dance," she instructed. "If it were one of the others, I could put a spell on her so that she wouldn't be afraid of making a mistake," she thought.

The lyres and the flutes and a little drum began to make music, and with Princess Medea leading we drifted out into the sunshine. We were birds, we were graceful, we swooped gently, our sandaled feet light in the meadow, our hair flying loose, and our pink robes floating as we turned and stepped.

When that was finished, such a roar went up from the Argonauts that it drowned out the music. The young lords were on their feet, cheering lustily and clapping.

When the noise stopped, we did Andromeda. I was Andromeda, in the middle where hardly anyone could see me. I didn't have to do anything but yearn with my arms to be rescued from a monster. There wasn't any monster, but everybody knows the story. All the other girls were Perseus, who did the rescuing.

The Argonauts roared even louder this time, and the serving women ran out with water jugs and cups so we could quench our thirst.

After that we were Nereids, sea goddesses swimming in air. The Argonauts were so noisy with their admiration that I judged it was a good idea not to have more than four dances if they were going to roar louder every time.

Feeling disgraced, because I couldn't be trusted in the final ribbon dance, I left Medea's doves and went back to Chalciope. I limped a little, preferring to have the audience think I had turned my ankle. I didn't want to admit the truth — that I was likely to tangle up the ribbons.

The dance was very pretty to watch. I nestled down near Chalciope when she beckoned.

"Did you turn your ankle?" she asked.

"No, my lady. But I'm not good in that dance. And the Lady Medea's spell of hypnotism doesn't work with me."

Chalciope looked thoughtful. "It doesn't?"

I was embarrassed. "She can make the others be clouds or lambs, but there is something wrong with me."

The ribbon dance finished, the roar went up again, and the Argonauts ran shouting out into the meadow. Armor made clinking sounds behind me as the spear guard got ready for trouble, but Chalciope quieted them with a gesture.

The King's guests were only escorting Medea and her maidens back to the shade, laughing and yelling compliments. In the lead, Jason walked beside Medea. Orpheus' voice went up in a song, and the other men joined in. The song was about Aphrodite, goddess of beauty and love.

That was a lovely time, after the dancing, with the handsome young lords paying us — even me — compliments under the tree, most of the girls blushing and everyone laughing and happy.

Orpheus shouted, "Where's the little one who hurt her ankle?" and came through the crowd to me. Blushing, I felt my cheeks get hot. He sat down beside me. "I'll cure that ankle," he promised, and began to strum his lyre.

He sang, in a low, sweet voice, with words that I could not understand at all. There was no sense in them, and I knew it was some kind of spell. If I had had any pain, it would surely have gone away.

"Does it hurt now?" he asked.

I answered truthfully, "Not at all, sir."

The first light of morning was coming through the high windows of our chamber when Medea entered, as soft-footed as the dawn, and awakened us, one by one. She

74

wore white, with a silvery veil over her hair. She carried a tiny metal box.

"Yoke the mules," she told us, "to the chariot of Hecate. You will go with me to her temple."

She showed us the box. "Here I have the ointment of Prometheus, made from flowers that sprang up where his first blood fell to earth."

We shivered, for we could guess at the terror that had gone into its making. That was one of the magic things that Medea had made, wandering alone in the mountains at night. The flowers grow in pairs on stalks as long as one's forearm, and the sap is deadly poison. She tucked the tiny box into the girdle around her slender waist.

We dressed hurriedly and ran to yoke the mules to her chariot. She drove the mules, and we tucked up our robes and ran beside the chariot, holding on to the wicker sides.

At the shrine of the goddess on the plain, Medea pulled up her team and stepped down from the chariot.

"Let us dance and sing and play games — and someone will come to see me," she said. "When he arrives, go away and leave me."

We danced for her, but there was no joy in it, and we sang with shrill, frightened voices. Then we saw three men coming: Chalciope's son Argeus and the Prophet Mopsus and Jason with the sun shining on his golden hair. We were glad enough to fall back so we could not hear and to turn so we could not see. Jason came forward alone to meet Medea.

The story we hear now about what happened next may be true; I do not know. But certainly many of the tales they tell about my poor lady now are dreadful lies. This is what the harpers sing:

Medea told Jason what he must do, and he did it. He sent two men to King Aeetes to get the dragon's teeth that had to be sowed like seed — they had been brought long before from faraway Thebes in Greece. That night Jason went alone to the dark plain, leading an ewe and carrying some milk and other things. He bathed in the river and put on a dark mantle. Then he dug a pit, put firewood in it, cut the ewe's throat, and laid the carcass on the wood. He set fire to the wood and poured libations, offering prayers to Hecate.

The Dark One herself arose, wearing a garland of living snakes, and the hounds of the underworld bayed fearfully, and the light of many torches glared while the meadow trembled. Jason, as he had been told to do, walked back to his ship, not looking behind him.

The palace was full of scurrying servants that night — no more of them around than usual, but all moving fast, spreading rumors in frightened whispers. The two princesses would cast powerful spells the next day, they said, to help Jason fight his awful battles.

The stories grew and grew: There really were live bulls made of brass — they had been seen, snorting fire. The girls in the common room became so frightened that they clustered in one corner and didn't want to go to bed. The servants scared each other too much to run around any more.

Tall Atalanta came striding in with a scowl on her sunburned face and demanded, "What is all this I hear about a spell?"

76

Rhoda answered her: "The Princesses have very powerful spells, my lady. Lady Medea often puts a spell on us — and no harm ever comes of it."

"Let me tell you," Atalanta said threateningly, "we'll all be armed tomorrow to fight with Jason if he needs it!"

Rhoda replied earnestly, "He will have the help of the Princesses, and he won't need any other."

"It sounds like nonsense to me," Atalanta growled. "There's treachery here."

She was obviously afraid, but being afraid never stopped the Argonauts. It was this very fear that would make them susceptible to the hypnotic spell.

The following morning a great crowd of frightened people gathered on the plain — many Colchians and all of Jason's men. News had spread through the city that danger threatened, so all the brave men came, and some women armed with knives and clubs, and those who weren't brave stayed home.

King Aeetes came in state, in his chariot, with his young son Apsyrtus driving, both wearing golden helmets.

Medea's maidens clustered together in a tight group and watched the foreigners take their positions. The Argonauts frowned and looked suspicious and did not let anyone with a weapon get behind them. I saw Atalanta with some of the other foreigners, armed and ready for a fight.

Doreen whispered, "They will start spearing people if Jason doesn't win."

I thought, "If Jason doesn't see what he is supposed to see, we'll all be dead."

77

Doreen remembered the names of some of the armed intruders. "That's Idas, the sullen-looking one. The older man is Polyphemus. The one with bulging muscles is Periclymenus — they say that in battle he can change his shape to confuse his enemies."

With them was a good-looking, hawk-faced boy, sixteen or seventeen years old, Meleager, the youngest of them all. Doreen sighed, "Isn't he wonderful?"

Elsa murmured, "Don't let the huntress see that he attracts you. She's jealous."

That was a startling thought. Atalanta was dedicated to the Virgin Goddess of Wild Things, so she could never marry, and she shouldn't have been interested in Meleager or any other man. Besides, she was several years older than he was.

Somewhere there was constant drumming, a sound like distant thunder that went into one's very blood. All through the day, the drumming never stopped.

The King's official herald came forward, carrying his staff of office with white ribbons on it, and bellowed:

"The Lord Jason has undertaken the tasks set for him by the King. Lord Jason will yoke fierce, fire-breathing bulls and plough the earth. Then he will plant the teeth of a frightful dragon that once threatened distant Thebes. From them will grow armed warriors. Lord Jason will strive to kill all the earthborn fighting men who spring from the furrows he ploughed. Then he will attempt to take the great golden fleece from the serpent that never sleeps!"

The audience moaned.

The herald continued: "King Aeetes shows his good

will toward the foreign guests by this: His own two daughters, the Princesses, will work their powerful spells to help Lord Jason!"

The audience cried out in a loud voice, shuddering, and Jason stepped forth, brandishing his shield and spear.

In the center of the great circle he stopped. He rubbed his shield and his weapons carefully all over with the ointment Medea had given him, and he rubbed the ointment on his own body to make him invulnerable. Then he leaped and danced while the sun glittered on the bronze of his armor.

On the top branch of a great bare tree, a shining bronze shield began to twist and turn. There was a man under the tree, pulling a rope.

Medea and Chalciope came forward, robed in black, and began to glide around the great circle, one to the right, one to the left. When they met, they stood back to back and cried to the people: "You must not stir from your places until we tell you Jason has conquered."

The two Princesses had had much experience in chanting at religious ceremonies. They could speak together so that the two voices sounded like one great melodious voice.

"Watch the shield, watch the shield turn," chanted the sisters, gliding. "Something will happen and you will see it."

When they did not chant, the plain was full of humming, as of bees. The people shuddered and moaned. Jason stood alone in the center of the circle, tense and waiting.

"The bulls are coming, you will see them. Breathing

fire, breathing flame," the sisters chanted. "There they come! There are the bulls!"

A great moan went up from the frightened audience, and those in the front ranks pushed back.

"Jason is fighting the bulls, Jason will tame them," came the shrill, monotonous chant. The sisters never slowed in their gliding, and the shield in the tree continued to twinkle and twist.

The Argonauts who stood near me kept scowling and rubbing their eyes. One with bulging muscles muttered to himself, not believing what others believed, not wanting to see it. Then he saw it and screamed.

80

Atalanta, suspicious and dangerous, saw it and screamed. Her weapons fell from her hands, and she collapsed on her face, writhing.

Suddenly I saw what was happening. The enchantment affected me too!

It was frightful. I saw the bronze-footed bulls breathing fire. I saw Jason meet them and twist them down by their horns. He yoked them to a plough and with great effort broke the field. I moaned with the others and shouted encouragement.

Then he picked up a helmet with the dragon's teeth in it and planted the furrows.

The meadow was full of noise, and beyond the shouting was the distant drumming, and all around us was the bee-like humming. The voices of Medea and her sister repeated, repeated, repeated what was happening before us.

"Jason is fighting the earth-born warriors," they said. "Jason is fighting the Sown Men."

He was slashing valiantly with his sword, thrusting and parrying, stabbing and conquering the frightful armed men who had grown up from the dragon's teeth.

When the last one fell, a triumphant shout arose. The Princesses screamed, "He has conquered them all! He has conquered them all! Jason has conquered!"

A mighty roar went up from the Plain of Ares: "Jason! Jason! Jason!"

7

The ploughing and the battle did not win the golden fleece for Jason. Those victories only gave him the right to try to take it from the Temple of Ares. The worship of Ares, the war god, was for men, and women seldom went to that shrine except in time of war, to pray for victory.

Rhoda told us: "The fleece there is like any fleece that has been hung in the river to collect flakes of gold, except that it is very large. It was dedicated so long ago that only the priest of the temple knows the full story — it was before his grandfather was born. No man has ever touched it since it was offered to the god.

"The Unsleeping Snake is of bronze. It was taken as war booty long ago, from some enemy city, and it is dedicated to Ares, too."

One of the girls shivered and asked, "How does this stranger dare to take the fleece that belongs to a god?"

Rhoda shook her head. "If Ares permits him to take it, then Ares does not want it any more. If Ares wants to keep the fleece, then perhaps something terrible will happen to Jason for profaning the shrine."

In the dark of night, Medea went with Jason to Ares'

temple. Everyone in the palace knew they were going, but everyone pretended not to know. We guessed what happened there.

She tried to persuade him not to commit the sacrilege of taking the fleece. She must have frightened him. But she could not stop him.

So she hypnotized him with the torchlight on the shining bronze of the Unsleeping Serpent so that it became tremendous and alive, twisting and hissing and threatening, and she sprinkled dried herbs on its eyes to make it sleep. It was necessary that Jason should believe he defeated the dragon.

He reached up with his spear and dragged the huge, dirty old fleece down from the wall, and then he ran, roaring, from the temple.

From the palace we could hear the triumphant shouting of his friends, and we saw their torches leap and blaze as they did a victory dance.

Medea came slowly back to the palace, a black shadow in the black night, and we all pretended not to know that she had saved Jason's life and was losing him forever.

Next morning we were all out of bed early — except Medea. She remained in her chamber and made no sound. This we knew — everyone in the palace knew it: The King had sternly commanded Medea never to see Jason again.

We could glimpse, through the corridor, palace servants scurrying, laden with bundles.

Rhoda remarked, "The King is very generous with guest-gifts as well as provisions for the ship's journey."

Elsa said, "Oh, I want to watch the ship when it leaves!"

The looms mistress said sharply, "You don't want to watch the ship. What you want — all you girls — is a last look at the foreign princes!"

We all laughed, because she was right. We pleaded, but she replied, "You'll not take even one step into the courtyard unless my lady gives permission — and you need not think I'm going to ask her."

At that moment we saw tall Atalanta lope through the corridor with a great bundle on her shoulder. She didn't look at us.

Doreen remarked, "Someone has been generous to the foreign lady, too. She had no baggage when she came."

We stood at our looms, dutifully weaving, listening to the noise in the courtyard. Elsa said, "Perhaps later in the day Medea will take us to the meadow."

But Medea never danced in that meadow again.

We were working, and trying to be cheerful about it, when Atalanta returned. This time she strode into the weaving room. She was ready for travel, bow in hand and quiver on shoulder.

She spoke solemnly, like an official herald: "The men of *Argo* ask that Medea come to the shore and give the ship the blessing of Hecate."

The looms mistress was so shocked that she dropped a lapful of blue-dyed wool. She gasped, "I can't disturb the Princess! Tell them that you could not give her the message."

"*I* can disturb her," Atalanta said gruffly, and went to Medea's door.

She said, "The Lord Jason implores Medea to pour a libation and pray for a safe passage through the dangers he must face."

There was no reply, and after a few minutes Atalanta went scowling out of the palace, not deigning to glance into the room where we worked.

A servant scurried in soon after that with news for the looms mistress — who had not yet given the mantle she had promised.

"All the auspices are bad!" the woman reported. "Some of the men servants say so. One of the foreigners — Melampus is his name — tried to get good omens for the journey by listening to what the birds say." She frowned. "Can anyone understand birds? I never heard of such a thing."

"Nobody should try," the looms mistress said primly. "It is not proper to ask the gods what the future holds.

The proper thing is to offer them praise and sacrifices and pray for their good will. Did the birds say anything?"

"Some wild doves were near, and whatever they said about the journey was bad," the woman reported. "So then Lord Mopsus tried. He put water in a silver basin and dropped olive oil on it, to see what shapes the oil drops would take and what they meant. But the meaning there was disastrous, too."

The looms mistress demanded, "Are they leaving, or aren't they?"

The servant, happy to be the center of attention, was in no hurry to answer that question. She said, "Then Mopsus shook a quiver of arrows until one fell out, and the markings on that one were unlucky. But they're going anyway, because the ship itself cried, 'Go.' Did you ever hear of a ship saying anything?"

"Ships creak," the looms mistress admitted. "But everybody says *Argo* does speak because a beam in it is made from a sacred tree."

The servant had just left the room when Medea was suddenly with us. We greeted her, and she nodded but did not speak. Her eyes looked as if she had been crying.

She walked around restlessly, glancing at the work we were doing. At last she spoke: "Has *Argo* left Colchis?"

"We do not know, my lady," the looms mistress answered. "But we heard that the omens are all bad — and that *Argo* must leave anyway."

Medea drew a deep breath. "I am going to the shore to ask the Dark One's blessing for the foreign lords."

The looms mistress cried out, "But the King ordered

86

you not to — " and clapped her hand over her mouth
and looked frightened, having spoken of something she
was not supposed to know.

Medea ignored her, saying only, "My maidens will
come with me. Doreen, carry the wine pitcher. Daphne,
bring the libation cup."

We formed a procession by twos and walked behind
the Princess. She was pale and silent. We were afraid,
because she was disobeying her father. But she was our
lady, and we did as she said.

Very few Colchians were at the launching place.
There were half a dozen servants, who had helped with
the loading, and a handful of off-duty guards. Prince
Apsyrtus and three or four of his friends were there, sitting on the ground and watching — thinking, no doubt,
how fine it would be to sail out to meet adventure. Some
smaller boys stood around warily, expecting to be chased
away.

The King and some of his nobles had been there in
state very early in the morning on a courtesy visit when
the Argonauts sacrificed a sheep to placate the sea god,
Poseidon, and to ask for a safe passage home. When that
was done, the ship was officially on its way, so only the
inquisitive who had nothing to do waited for its actual
departure.

Argo floated gently on the quiet water, attached with
only one stout rope to the slanting platform used for
loading and boarding. The foreign heroes were on board,
most of them in their places at the oars, each with his
shield protecting him from the side. The men looked
disconsolate. Jason and three or four others were bend-

ing over something that, we assumed, was supposed to promise them good fortune instead of bad.

Rhoda went to the foot of the platform and announced, "The priestess of Hecate will ask the goddess for a safe journey for the guests of King Aeetes."

A shout of joy went up from the Argonauts. Jason leaped to the head of the platform, smiling a welcome at Medea. We girls stared. I wanted one last look at Orpheus, and the others had their favorites, of course.

Medea, without saying a word, turned her back to the ship and motioned for me to hold the shallow cup so that Doreen could pour wine into it. Then the Princess looked up at Jason — the last look she would ever have at him, she thought.

He spoke formally: "Jason, son of Aeson, asks the priestess to board *Argo* and pour the libation on the fabric of the ship itself, for *Argo* is our only hope of safe return."

Medea hesitated. Then, without a word, she started up the slanting platform to comply.

Suddenly I had a fearful vision. I saw Medea in a place where the darkness of night was slashed with leaping flames and black smoke swirled around her and she was herself very dreadful.

Appalled, I cried out, "My lady!" and dropped the libation cup, and it shattered.

Medea screamed. She whirled and slapped me.

There was a blur of action. Jason seized Medea as if she were a feather and ran with her up the platform and leaped down into the ship. Without thinking of anything but to plead with her to forgive my awkwardness with the cup, I sped after her.

Atalanta scooped me off the platform with one strong arm, twitched loose the mooring rope with the other hand, and stood erect, laughing.

Two or three of the surprised and bewildered Argonauts shouted questions: "What's this about? . . . That's the King's daughter!"

A great cry of anger went up from those on shore. The soldiers hurled their spears at *Argo*, and those with bows shot their arrows, but the foreigners were protected by their shields.

"Row!" shouted Jason. "Strike and pull!"

Astonished as they were, the Argonauts were disciplined, and they were in danger, so their oars struck the water as if the ship were a living thing with long arms that moved together from one body.

Atalanta ducked to avoid the arrows, and in her swift movement dropped me down into the hull. As I fell, I had a glimpse of Apsyrtus leaping on a horse to gallop for help. My head struck something, and for a while I was unconscious.

I awakened with a headache and a sick feeling that everything in the world was suddenly wrong. Medea was holding me on her lap, but she was not looking at me. She was staring at Atalanta with slitted eyes, and she was frowning, so I knew she was not afraid.

The noise was terrible — the men in the ship were shouting, and the oars were creaking as the foreign princes pulled to a cadence pounded out by someone at the

89

back. There were thuds as arrows or spears from shore struck the Argonauts' shields.

I spoke into Medea's ear: "My lady, I didn't mean to ruin the libation! I had a foreseeing."

"It was not your fault," she replied. "Atalanta is to blame, I think."

I crouched beside my princess — she was sitting regally on a bale of baggage — and I shivered, watching her hands. They moved like serpents' heads as she cast a spell at Atalanta, who lounged against the mast, showing her white teeth in a sneering smile.

I expected to see her shrivel and die under the curse of Medea, but she did not. She shouted, above the noise, "Don't be a fool. If you weren't in love with Jason, you wouldn't have come down to see him leave!"

Medea's hands went on moving, and her lips moved with strange words that I could not understand.

We could not see what was happening on shore, but there were no longer any treetops above us. I had never been in a ship before — and if the gods are willing I'll never set foot in a ship again. *Argo* was very large. She had to be large to accommodate so many rowers and their supplies and belongings. We were down in the bottom, where there was a narrow platform to keep things from getting wet with the water that sloshed around. Bales of cargo were roped to the platform.

The Argonauts were a little above us on benches, pulling their great oars, each man with his shield fastened beside him to keep off arrows and spears.

The ship began to toss, and Medea, her spell finished, said, "Now we are in the open sea!"

90

The Black Sea, we called it in Colchis, but the Argonauts called it the Lucky Sea, hoping to persuade it to treat them kindly. Now that we were in the wind, some of the men put up the sail, and then we seemed to move very fast.

The movement was dreadful — the ship was a live thing, leaping forward. I had never been in even a tiny boat. I had never set eyes upon the sea and had not wanted to and could not see it now. I shuddered and clung to Medea.

"What was the foreseeing?" she asked after a long time.

"I don't want to tell you, my lady," I replied.

"You must. There may be help in it, for the present or the future. That is what foreseeings are for, you know. Tell me, Daphne."

"Smoke and fire in the night, my lady — and you in the midst of it, tall and frightful."

Medea laid her hand on my aching head. Her golden eyes looked into mine. "Remember more," she commanded. "Remember all of it."

"Terror around you — but you are in control of those who hate you. How could anyone hate my lady?"

I began to cry.

"That is to come," she said. "It is well to be warned. Remember more. Remember all of it."

"Your arms are moving. You are casting a spell."

"What did you hear, Daphne? Remember all of it."

"A deep booming sound, and the flashing of flames on metal — as it was when you and your sister helped Jason in the meadow. And that is all, my lady."

"No sound from the fire? No crackling from the flames?"

"No sound but the dreadful booming and your voice, and another voice, too. I didn't want to tell you! It is dreadful to think about."

"But the foreseeing may save my life some day," she said quietly. "I think that was its purpose."

Late that night, after dark, the men took down the sail and rowed *Argo* into a cove and pulled her up on shore. Jason came over the piled cargo and bowed to Medea and said, "Lady, I did not plan it this way! May I help you up the ladder?"

She did not seem to hear him or to see his outstretched hand. But when one of the other lords offered his hand, she left the ship, and I followed.

The men made camp and prepared our evening meal, some of them always keeping a lookout for pursuing ships. Medea refused food. I stayed near her and did not sleep very much, but I think she did not sleep at all. She stared at the moon and murmured.

Everyone was afraid of Medea by the end of the second day, when we pulled up at another island. Nobody tried to talk to her any more. The princes looked away when she turned her golden eyes on them.

There was much worried talk among them, because the King's navy was pursuing us. The ships of Colchis were searching on the face of the sea for the King's daughter.

On the third day we did not travel at all. Most of the Argonauts were very sick, too weak to row. At the end of the day, Jason tried to speak to Medea, but she seemed not to hear him. She took out her little golden ball and began to twirl it. He covered his eyes with his arm and turned away. He staggered and was very pale, being deathly sick.

After a while the prophet Mopsus came, but not to Medea. He approached humbly and made a gesture of respect to me, although I was nobody important.

"My companions implore the Princess to lift her evil spell," he said. "We have been poisoned."

"If you have been poisoned," I replied, "it was not by the Princess. She has no drugs with her. She has nothing at all."

He nodded. "By her father, then. Only those of us who did not eat meat yesterday are well today. Please tell the Princess that we will build her an altar to sacrifice to the goddess on our behalf."

I went to Medea and gave her the message. She held out her empty hands in a hopeless gesture but did not speak.

"The Princess was taken captive," I reminded Mopsus. "She has none of the things that the goddess expects her priestess to use in a ceremony of worship."

Mopsus beckoned to Atalanta, who came over, looking ashamed, with a great bundle, and said gruffly, "I brought her things when I left the palace." She handed me the bundle, and I let it drop, being afraid to hold the sacred objects.

"You stole them from the shrine inside the palace!" I gasped.

Atalanta said crossly, "It's too late to argue about it now," and turned away.

My lady beckoned for me to go with her to a grove where nobody could see us. There she unwrapped the bundle. First she took out the objects pertaining to worship, and one of them she let me see — a sandal made of brass.

Her ivory box of poisons and healing drugs was there, and so were several of her finest robes and even some of her jewelry. She spoke quietly:

"She could not have brought these things without bribing a servant. The servant will die."

"From an evil spell, my lady?"

"No. My father will have her killed. But more mercifully," Medea added thoughtfully, "than he will punish me if I go home."

I shuddered. "But they captured you! They took you against your will!"

"Nevertheless, I disobeyed the King when I left the palace to offer a prayer for the ship's safekeeping on the sea . . . The servant who was bribed must have ransacked the palace shrine. That folded robe, all trimmed with gold — it is ancient and has a spell on it. I have never touched it."

"It is a beautiful robe, fit for a queen," I said.

"It is so old that nobody remembers whether the spell was for fortune or evil. It was kept in a chest in the shrine for generations before my father went to Colchis. Never touch it."

It would have been better if the robe had been thrown into the fire. Years later it brought pain and death to a young princess whom Medea had never heard of when

94

we stood in the grove that day. And it brought terrible blame to Medea herself.

The Argonauts, although they were still weak and sick, built a suitable altar for Medea's use, and she went, clothed in black, into the grove for the ceremony that no one could watch. She was smiling as she glided, swiftly and with seeming eagerness, as Hecate required.

Now she is afraid, for she smiles, I understood.

Through all the terrors that beset us from then on, Medea almost always smiled, even when the lords and heroes themselves were weak with fear. They could admit it. She could not, so thoroughly disciplined was she.

8

WHILE MEDEA was in the grove, those of the Argonauts who weren't too sick to talk held council, not caring that I heard.

It is said that never before in all the world were there gathered so many bold, courageous, lordly adventurers as the Argonauts. What is not said is that whatever they wanted they took, from a peasant's pig to a king's daughter. Those of them who are still alive are still boasting, I am sure, about the terrible things they did on their way to Colchis and back.

A man must have pride, of course, but these lords and kings had so much arrogant pride that the gods were offended and punished them. There is no other explanation for the miseries they had to endure — and us with them.

They were a quarrelsome lot, quick to take offense. In their own countries each of them was accustomed to being more important than almost everybody else, but on this voyage they were equals. They had a bitter quarrel before they ever launched *Argo* to seek the golden fleece.

In formal councils, a man could speak only when he

held the official staff in his hand, and nobody was supposed to interrupt the speaker. (They did, though, with growls or shouts of "No!")

When a speaker finished, he passed the staff on to the next man designated by the council leader — Jason, usually — and after much oratory they voted on a course of action by holding up their swords and yelling. While they argued, their swords were all laid in a heap for the sake of safety.

At this council I did not yet know the names of everyone who spoke.

One said, "It is the Princess that the Colchians want. Leave her here and let them have her!"

Another argued, "No, they want the golden fleece — and that they cannot have."

Atalanta took the staff — she never wanted to be left out of any argument — and said, "Oh, leave the King's daughter here. She'll only be a burden to us."

One of the men growled, "Nobody invited *you*, lady," and she glared and grabbed at the place where her sword would have hung if she hadn't taken it off.

She continued, "We can find a king around here somewhere to arbitrate with her father — let him judge whether she should go back."

I was shocked, because Jason did not object to that idea. But Orpheus did, eloquently. With the staff in his right hand, he cried, "Let the Princess starve on this island or help the farmers' wives glean the grain? Or be captured by her father's men and returned to him while we're searching for a judge? Her father would kill her. She did disobey him."

A few others agreed with Orpheus, but most of them sided with Atalanta. Medea was now only a foreign girl who had become a danger to them.

When Medea came out of the grove, she put the ivory box on the big flat rock and laid green leaves in a pattern around it. She paced three times around the rock, chanting and moving her hands, then three times in the opposite direction. The Argonauts stared and shivered.

She stood still then and looked directly at me, and it was as if she told me what to do although she did not speak or beckon.

I went to the cooking place and took a small clay bowl and dipped hot water from the brass caldron by the fire. Then I knelt before her, holding the bowl. She chanted as she dropped herbs into it.

The odor of them took me for a moment back to my father's hut, because this was the same medicine that my mother gave us children when we were sick from eating bad food. But my mother did not use any spells, and I realized that the Princess did not need them either.

She kept chanting until the water had cooled. Then she carried the bowl in both hands and offered it first to Jason, because he was the leader of the Argonauts. He hesitated a long time, staring up at her. He reached for the bowl.

Atalanta cried, "No! She's a witch!" and some of the men cried warning, too, but Jason drank the potion anyway. Nobody ever said he wasn't a brave man. And perhaps he, too, remembered the odor of those healing herbs.

She offered it to each of those who were sick. Some

of them drank — Orpheus was one of them — and some shuddered and waved the bowl away before it was close enough for them to smell the familiar odor of the helpful potion.

The next morning, those who had dared to drink were well, but the others continued sick and weak for several days. Miserable as they were, they had to work the ship or be caught and slaughtered by the King's navy.

They were worried about which way to sail. They spoke of a prophecy: They had been told that they would not return to their own lands the same way they had come. So they had to choose a direction.

They put a blindfold on one of their number, chosen by lot, and he whirled until he was dizzy. Then he pointed — and in that direction a shooting star sank through the night sky.

"A sign! A sign!" they shouted. That was the direction *Argo* would take when she set sail the next morning.

During the night I told Medea of the decision they had made, to desert her on the island. She answered gently, "Thank you for warning me."

In the morning, when the men gathered formally to tell her what they had decided, she did not seem to notice — but she heard.

Jason spoke: "Princess, the men of *Argo* have considered our situation. We are all in danger — you, too."

Medea gazed at the sea.

"The ships of Colchis are all around us," Jason said. "If your father's navy finds us, we are doomed. Even my strong comrades cannot win a battle against all those ships and men."

No answer from Medea.

"You will be much safer if you are separated from us," Jason continued. "This island is sacred to your goddess. Nobody will harm you here."

Medea smiled. (I stared at Jason with such disgust that he should have felt it like a fire.)

"You know I want to marry you, Princess Medea," Jason went on, becoming embarrassed. "But for your own safety's sake we must leave you here for a while. We will seek a neutral kingdom and ask the king to judge whether you should go back to Colchis or come on to our homeland. That is what we have decided." He stepped back and drew a deep breath of relief, having said what he had to say.

Medea's voice was music as she answered, "I have heard, Lord Jason."

Gracefully, without hesitation, she knelt before him.

"You are my lord now," she said. "My father would kill me after terrible torments, because my disobedience has caused deaths among his people.

"My brother Apsyrtus is leading the pursuit. I had a farseeing — he is on the flagship. It is not far away. Send someone to parley with him, I implore you. Take him gifts and ask him to command the navy to let *Argo* go in safety.

"And I will go with you and these other lords, away from my own country forever, to avoid another battle. And I will be your wife and queen in your own kingdom."

An approving murmur went up from the Argonauts, crowding all around to listen. Jason looked around and saw their faces. Then he took Medea's hand and lifted her to her feet and kissed her.

That night a messenger went in a small boat, one of the men who lived on the island, and took the word to the flagship. My lady did not sleep that night. She sat on a rock, smiling, while I dozed against her knee.

No one explained anything to us, but toward morning the messenger returned, and the Argonauts took up their arms and went down to the shore, carrying bundles of rich parley-gifts for Prince Apsyrtus. We heard shouts in the distance.

In the morning they came back. Jason said briefly, "He refused. But the flagship has gone, and we will sail at once."

The harpers tell of the places where the Argonauts went and the perils they passed through and the battles they fought. Some of this is true, and some is a poet's golden lie or the echo of a returned traveler's boast.

Safe now in this foreign land, I listen and remember.

I remember the seas and the islands and the strange rivers, broad and placid or narrow and treacherous, and the vast prairies and the great forests where mountains sloped down to the banks. I remember the long terror and the cold, the hunger and the thirst and the sun's blazing heat. And I remember the ship named *Argo*.

Argo had a small platform at each end for the steersman and the lookout and the cadence gong and such things. There was no privacy except for a tiny room under one platform with a leather curtain in front of it.

The rowers could look over the sides if they didn't need their shields braced to protect them from enemy

missiles. But the cargo and we two unwilling passengers from Colchis were down in the hull. We could see only up, and there was seldom anything there except the sky and clouds.

Argo, to us, was a long wooden pit.

The Argonauts had all kinds of nautical names for parts of the ship. I ignored them all. So did Medea. The planks in the bottom were supposed to be called the deck, Atalanta informed me haughtily. I went right on calling them the floor.

The floor was stacked with baggage and bedding and trade goods and treasure and food supplies and cooking pots and jars of wine and water, neatly stacked or nestled and tied down.

But sometimes a knot did not hold and something slid. Or someone stumbling from one end of the ship to the other lost his balance and went flying. Or a man sleeping on a pile of baled cargo would roll off. Most of us had bruises most of the time. During storms it was even worse.

There was a great deal of food in the ship, thanks to the generosity of King Aeetes. There was grain and cured beef and stacks of bread and jars of raisins and nuts and honey. There were axes for trading with barbarians — but the Argonauts were more likely to take what they wanted than to trade something for it. There were great pieces of copper, as long as your arm and the shape of an oxhide — heavier than I could lift — and worth a cow. These were used for trading with barbarian tribes that needed metal.

The most precious thing in that cargo was fire. That was kept in a big metal caldron with charcoal, and the Argonauts were very careful to renew the fuel each time we landed. Each day we sailed, two men were appointed to care for the fire. It had to be kept covered so that water could not get in and quench it, but not covered so tightly that it could not breathe.

When the wind was against us or when there wasn't a wind, the Argonauts rowed — two men to each oar. But when the leather sail was on the mast and the wind carried us in the direction they wanted to go, they climbed down from the benches and clambered over the bales and bundles, stretching and talking and making plans — and either laughing or quarreling.

They argued about details of their perilous adventures and about whose kingdom raised the finest sheep or

grapes or grain. They argued about their illustrious an-
cestors and about battles that their great-grandfathers
had won or lost. They blamed one another for anything
that went wrong, and each one took the credit for all
their successes.

The only thing that kept them from hitting one another oftener than they did was that the ship was too
crowded, and when they pulled *Argo* to shore at night
they were too hungry and tired.

After a few days I could name almost all the lords.
They looked very different now, with their hair blowing
and their beards untrimmed and their short working
clothes smudged and ragged, from the way they looked
at the presentation in the King's palace.

Two of them had the same name, Ancaeus. Big Ancaeus was the helmsman. He usually steered the ship.
Little Ancaeus was a surly man, always accusing someone of something.

The lookout was named Lynceus. He had such sharp
eyes that he could keep watch even during darkness.
When we sailed sometimes at night, he slept in the daytime. He could even see ghosts, and he would not sleep
in the fore part of the ship where a terrible oxhide bundle was stowed. That was the bundle that held the bones
of Phrixus, which the Argonauts had stolen from the
funeral grove.

Meleager was not a grown man yet, but he was tall and
strong and did his share of the rowing and other hard
work. Atalanta was always hovering where he was and
trying to look after him. He often acted annoyed at her

attentions. Maybe she was only being a big sister to him, but he didn't want a sister.

They had their troubles, the men of *Argo*, but the only one who had any sympathy from me was Orpheus the sweet singer. He mourned for his wife Euridice, who had died from the sting of a poisonous serpent on the very day of their wedding.

Atalanta told me that he had actually dared to go down to the terrible House of the Dead to bring her back, but on the way back to the House of the Living, he turned to see if she were following and thus lost her again completely.

Euphemus, a son of the sea god, was the best swimmer in the whole crew. He was like a dolphin in the water. He was a swift runner, too, and Atalanta was jealous of him.

Argus, builder of the ship, was always fussing about some repair or other. He was vastly proud of his handiwork but full of second thoughts. He kept saying, "Now if I had it to do over — "

The planks were fastened with strong pegs and bound with ropes and roots, which had to be inspected often and sometimes replaced.

In our journeying, Hecate the moon waxed and waned four times, and the season changed and the winds grew wild and cold.

Not only the season changed. My lady changed, too. She could not do otherwise. She was only a mortal girl, and she could never go home again. In our camping places she would sit beside Jason and let him tell how she would be queen in his country when he gained the throne that his uncle had usurped. Sometimes they walked together on the shore, hand in hand.

9

THE ARGONAUTS were often kind to us, regretting what had happened. Orpheus was especially thoughtful of my comfort. He soothed me when I was afraid.

Once while he was playing his lyre and singing, a young deer came trotting out of the woods. Atalanta seized her bow, but Medea cried, "No, go back!" and the deer whirled and fled.

Orpheus put down his lyre, remarking, "My lady, I did not know that you have power over wild things."

"It is proper," Medea answered. "The deer is beloved of Hecate."

"And of Artemis, another name for the goddess," he said. "Now I'll invite him to come back."

He played and sang, and the deer returned. It trotted to me — Orpheus must have commanded it — and let me pet its nose. Then it went to Medea, and she whispered to it, and it lay down at her feet.

"There are other beasts in the forest," Orpheus said. "Listen and watch."

He played harsher music, and a great spotted cat creature appeared at the edge of our camping place. The young deer pricked up its big ears but did not leap away.

As Orpheus went on singing, the great cat padded cautiously across the grass, obeying the sweet singer. It lay down at Medea's feet, too, and licked the deer once as a sign of friendship.

"Dismiss them, lady," Orpheus said.

Medea made a gesture, and the animals bounded away in opposite directions.

That is one of the good things I remember, the way Orpheus could calm fear. All of us were afraid sometimes.

The fear increased, because none of the Argonauts knew where we were or where we were going or even how to get back to the sea. We stayed at one camp for three days while scouts went out to climb up high places and get the lay of the land.

108

We went on another river, into another sea, and a howling gale caught *Argo* and shook the ship in its teeth. Medea and I huddled together, as the men and Atalanta rowed and the helmsman, Ancaeus, roared the cadence of the stroke, with his voice beating through the sound of the wind and the creaking of the vessel.

Argo's timbers groaned and cried out in pain. The ship writhed and twisted.

Medea screamed, "Listen!"

Jason cried out, for he had heard something too.

Ancaeus roared, "Up oars! Up oars!" and the rowers pulled their blades out of the surging water.

Night was falling. We seldom traveled in darkness. Such travel is dangerous for all seafaring men, even when they are not lost in unfamiliar waters. But this gale was so fierce that the steersman could not choose his course to seek shelter on shore or at an island.

Ancaeus clambered from one rower to another, yelling instructions. When he was just above where we sat, I heard fragments of what he said:

"At the beat, hold fast. . . . beat, hold fast. . . . three, up oars. . . . up oars."

It made no sense to me. I clung to the princess, and we trembled. I was glad it was too dark for me to see her smile. There was neither moon nor stars, nothing but scudding darkness.

There was movement near us, and somebody stumbled over my foot. Then right beside us, two strong voices rose on the wind:

"O Father, O North Wind, hear now your sons!"

They chanted together and then separately, asking

North Wind to be gentle, to save his sons and their ship-
mates and their ship. They were Zetes and Calais, whose
sandals had bronze wings at the back.

The wind did seem to slacken a little; then it howled
again.

A man's hand seized my arm, and his voice yelled in
my ear, "Daphne, I need you. I am Big Ancaeus." He
led me, stumbling, across the spray-wet bales and bundles.

He boosted me up to the little deck aft, and in the
darkness he shouted to another Argonaut, "Melampus,
son of Poseidon, beseech your father who rules the
sea!"

Melampus slid down into the wooden pit. He had
been beating cadence on the small deck, but now he had
something more important to do. The rowers did not
need him anyway. They were idle on their oars but still
alert in their places.

As Ancaeus seated me on a small bench, out of the
wind, I heard the voice of Melampus rise through the
wind in a kind of counterchant to the voices of the North
Wind's sons: "Father Poseidon, hear now your son Melampus! Calm these waves, we beseech you!"

Ancaeus yelled in my ear: "Here is the cadence gong,
and here is the mallet." He closed my hand around it.
"When I slap your shoulder once, beat the gong once,
hard. If I slap three times, beat three times. You understand?"

I did, and very soon he slapped once, and I swung the
mallet and struck the gong one blow.

The ship almost swamped. The beat was a signal for

an experiment: The rowers dipped their oars to try to slow *Argo* in her course, but perhaps they did not have complete control or could not see what they were doing and did not all do it together. *Argo* swerved and swooped.

Ancaeus yelled and beat my shoulder three times, and I swung the mallet three times — and we were at least no worse off than before the experiment, except a little wetter, for this was a signal for the oars to be lifted.

After a long time, morning came, and the sea was not so rough and the wind was not so fierce. And there was an island. Ancaeus told me when to beat cadence so the rowers could bring the ship into a harbor out of the wind. But for a long time after the ship was beached and fires were built and the weary Argonauts were stretched out, too tired to unload, the solid earth still seemed to swing and jolt.

As we shivered by the fire, Jason spoke to the company:

"*Argo* spoke. Did you hear?"

Several of the men answered, "I heard." Some shook their heads, puzzled.

"What did you hear?" he demanded. His teeth were chattering.

Mopsus answered: "The talking beam of sacred oak said, 'Great Zeus is angry. You will have no peace until Jason and Medea are purified of blood guilt.'"

My lady clutched my hand and pressed against me.

"Some men died because of me," she said. "Drowned, or in battle."

Mopsus glanced at Jason and said bluntly, "There is

more guilt than that, my lady. The blood of your brother is on Jason's hands — and on yours."

Medea screamed — a long, terrible, warbling sound that still chills my blood when I remember.

Jason stood with his back to us, clenching his fists and shuddering.

"It is true," he said. "Apsyrtus came to the meeting place. We fought — and I killed him."

"We can never cross that stormy sea," said Zetes. "The winds of Zeus forbid it." We had to believe him, for this was one of the Sons of the North Wind who spoke.

His brother added, "We are accursed, all of us, and the ship, too, until the guilt can be cleansed."

"But how?" groaned Jason. "How? No mortal can lift that curse!"

Euphemus said, "At the sacred place at Dodona, where *Argo*'s talking beam was hewed from the oak tree that talks, Zeus gives the power to his priests."

But where was Dodona? Where were we? Lost, after journeying on strange rivers and into an unfriendly sea.

Phanus said, "At Delphi, where Apollo speaks to men, the curse could be lifted. But where is Delphi? Where are the shores we know?"

Medea had sat mourning as the men talked. Now she unveiled her face and said, "My father's sister, Circe, has the power from their father Helios the sun — you call him Apollo. She lives on an island in the Great Sea. But I do not know where it is." She cried out, "None of us know where we are!"

Orpheus was fingering his lyre. He began to sing in a

soothing way: "We must go on. We can go on. Take heart, my friends. Courage ebbs like the tide, but the tide grows full again."

Out of the darkness came two fluttering creatures like birds, straight at Medea. They swooped down and rested on her shoulders. They were bats, creatures of the darkness. Medea did not try to frighten them away, because bats are the birds of Hecate.

"An omen!" Mopsus exclaimed. "A promise from the Dark Goddess! We must go on — we can go on."

All their strong voices joined with that of Orpheus to sing the courage song.

We did go on. We passed along a fearsome river rimmed with walls of stone where monsters made of stone crouched as if to spring.

The men rowed down this river, helped by the current. The wind was wrong for sailing and would have dashed us against the cliffs. Orpheus noticed that I was shivering, fearful of the stone monsters, and he said, "They are not real, and no man made them. The wind and the water did it, I think."

I looked at him gratefully — and suddenly I saw not Orpheus but something terrible. We were on another river, and the woods on both sides of it were blazing with fire. Some furry animal — a fox, I thought — came running through the fire and leaped into the water with its fur in flames.

I screamed and startled all the ship's company. Medea seized my hand and asked, "Is it a farseeing?"

I hid my face against her shoulder and answered, "A

river with fire on both sides — a terrible place."

Atalanta turned around, scowling, and yelled, "It is enough that we have one witch on board *Argo*! Now the little girl is trying to be a witch too!"

Jason asked what had frightened me, and after I explained he asked Mopsus and Orpheus whether they had any omens of danger. They had not felt anything, but Mopsus said, "It may be true anyway, you know. We can't go back. We must go forward."

The others agreed, and Atalanta looked disgusted every time she glanced at me.

The next day we smelled smoke, faintly, and the day after that we came into the fire — suddenly, with the river narrowing and its swift current whirling us along.

"Back stroke! Back stroke!" roared the helmsman — but it was no use. There was not room enough for those long oars to bite deeply into the river. There was not strength enough in the rowers' arms to force *Argo* back against the current.

We strangled in the choking smoke and cringed before the roar and heat of the flames. I dipped my mantle in water in the bottom of the ship and threw it over Medea's head and huddled with her under it. The others seized any piece of fabric they could reach — and the sheepskins used for bedding as well — and soaked them and used them for protection. There was a great deal of yelling and the crackling of the burning trees. Even Orpheus was too busy to sing about courage. We huddled in the bottom of the hull while the ship swept on, unguided.

We had some burns afterward. There is a scar on my foot. But we lived through the fire and the smoke, and that evening when we were safe on a sandy shore, the Princess soothed our burns with her herbs while I held the dish. One of Atalanta's braids was shorter than the other because a piece of flying bark had burned her hair.

How I hated to see Medea kneeling before that woman! But one of her obligations was to care for the sick and injured.

We drifted through a forest where the trees wept sap. They were nymphs mourning, my lady said. They were daughters of Helios the sun, her own relatives.

We had to find another of his daughters, Circe. The ship and all its company were accursed until she could be found and persuaded to purify Jason and Medea.

More than once we came near destruction. We were lost and sometimes hungry. In these strange lands the people were wild men who did not plant crops. The supplies brought from Colchis were long gone. We had wild game for meat and fish from the rivers, but we longed for the olives and cheese and grain and onions of civilized places. We hungered for fruit but found only tasteless berries.

We were caught once in a marsh without end, stinking and clutching — a slow river took us there in a heavy fog, and a whole day of rowing took us back to the river and clean air that we gulped into our lungs.

We saw great beasts, and the men never moved far from their weapons. A bear licked Medea's hand but growled at the rest of us.

Sometimes we glimpsed savage people who wore animal skins or went naked except for their own fur. They cast rocks or crude spears at us and ran away, roaring.

Medea was no longer white of skin with silken hair. Her skin was dark and rough with wind and sun. I could not smooth her hair properly any more, because we had lost the comb.

But she was still Medea, sometimes sullen, sometimes serene. She kept track of the phases of the moon and carried out her obligations to Hecate with small sacrifices and chanted prayers, always alone in some dark grove, as was required. The forests were alive with dangerous beasts, but no beast harmed Medea.

When Medea turned away from the blown smoke of the cooking fire, wrapped in a mantle that was ragged now, she might have been a peasant's daughter — except for her golden eyes.

The young lords were strong and skilled with weapons — watching them practice with sword and spear and protecting shield, you would have thought nothing could defeat them. They were swift in foot races and strong in wrestling. Even when they were in danger, they laughed often, in the joy of being strong.

But they had their fears and sorrows. Peleus is one whom I remember well. He often walked alone beside the sea or stared at the waves from his rowing bench in *Argo*, as if watching for something.

One evening I spoke of this to Orpheus, who was putting a new string on his lyre. He had made the string from a dried tendon of a wild pig that he killed with a swift arrow.

116

"The Lord Peleus," I said, "seems always to be watching for something in the sea."

"Yes, his wife," Orpheus answered, tightening the string and listening to the sound as he plucked it. "She is Thetis. She left him in anger and plunged into the sea."

"She drowned?" I asked in horror.

Orpheus smiled. "Oh, no, for she is a Nereid. She and her sisters live in the sea. Peleus mourns because he lost her. Their son, Achilles, is being educated by old Chiron the Centaur in a cave on Mount Olympus now. I'll sing you the story, shall I?"

Plucking the strings of his lyre, he sang the sad story of how Peleus lost his wife.

Thetis was a goddess, and her wedding to Peleus had been fine indeed. All the Divine Ones attended, and great Hera herself, the wife of Zeus, carried the bridal torch in the procession. But the goddess of Discord was not invited, and she made great trouble. She came to the wedding anyway and tossed a golden apple on the ground and cried, "For the fairest!"

Three great goddesses competed for the prize, and the judge was a mere mortal, a prince named Paris from a city named Troy. Hera promised him riches if he would name her the fairest. Athena, goddess of wisdom, promised him wisdom and victory in war. Aphrodite, the laughing goddess of love, promised him the most beautiful of mortal women.

Prince Paris awarded the golden prize to Aphrodite.

When a son was born to Thetis and Peleus, they named him Achilles, and his mother undertook to make him immortal so that he would never die. Every night, when her husband was sleeping, she rubbed the baby's body with ambrosia and held him in the fire to purge away mortality. She had almost finished with this rite when Peleus awoke one night and saw her holding the baby by one ankle over the fire and chanting the spell that would make him live forever, like the gods.

Peleus shouted with horror, and Thetis dropped the baby on the floor and dashed out of the palace and dived into the sea, screaming that he had spoiled everything.

"Your son will die before you!" she prophesied. "But he will be greater than his father. His name will live forever on the lips of men."

Orpheus laid down his lyre and said, "So you see why Peleus watches the waves. He is looking for his lost and lovely Thetis."

"And who is the most beautiful woman in the world that the prince from Troy will marry? Surely there is no one more beautiful than the Lady Medea."

Orpheus laughed. "I have never seen anyone who was, but Castor and Polydeuces have a little sister named Helen, back in Sparta. They say she will be the most beautiful woman in the world."

Peleus was not the only Argonaut who was sometimes sad. Mopsus the prophet was another. He knew that he would die from the sting of a serpent, so although he was a brave man he was very much afraid of snakes. Sometimes Medea picked up a snake and fondled it and talked to it. Poor Mopsus turned pale, and his teeth chattered when he watched her.

Some days were pure enchantment. One sunny day, as *Argo* sped before the wind, Orpheus sang:

"Comrades, remember! You came safely through perils. You will come through others. Comrades, remember!"

A flight of seabirds swooped from the blue sky and sailed just above us on slanting wings, and the ship's company joined voices and sang, "Comrades, remember!"

The rowers were relaxed and resting, not stumbling around or arguing about anything. All went well — until suddenly a cloud obscured the sun and the seabirds fled, screaming, and a chill came into our hearts.

Medea said in a voice of wonder, "We are almost there!"

Mopsus the prophet answered, "I feel it too."

The lookout shouted, "Land ho! An island!"

And the helmsman cried out, "The wind has not changed, but we are sailing directly toward that island, no matter how I try to move the steering oar!"

10

AND so we came to Circe's island, and we were all afraid.

She was kneeling on the shore, dipping her long golden hair in the sea and tossing it back, wailing incantations.

Near her huddled pitiful, hideous creatures. I saw a great dog with the face of a man, and a man with a boar's head and curving tusks. Tears ran down its cheeks.

There was a thing like a bear that did not shamble, as a bear does, but walked on cat's feet. It cried out with the voice of a woman: "The walls of your house stream with blood, Circe!"

Circe wailed, "Blood!"

As *Argo* drew in, Orpheus smiled kindly at those horrors and struck his lyre softly. The monsters sat on the shore, entranced by his music.

Medea spoke quietly: "Daphne, I want you to come with me. Bring with you this small bundle, pretending it is a gift for Circe."

I took the bundle, wondering. Later I learned that it contained Medea's box of magic drugs and the objects sacred to the Dark Goddess.

The Princess went on: "You and I will stay here with my father's sister if she will permit it."

I did not let her know that I was shivering at the thought. To live among those beasts on shore — who could endure it?

But there were girls there, too, several of them, Circe's handmaidens. They did not seem afraid. Their faces were empty and stupid looking.

When Circe stood up, dripping, with her feet in the sea, two of the girls waded out and then swam toward *Argo*, calling, "Come ashore! Come ashore!"

Jason looked terror-stricken as he turned toward the ship's company and made a gesture that said, "No!"

He spoke: "Medea will go with me to talk to Circe. No one else."

Medea said lightly, "Daphne will come with me, of course. I have a gift for my father's sister, and it would not be proper for me to carry the bundle."

The Argonauts were glad enough to stay at their oars. The ship gently rocked in the shallow water as Jason helped us down.

Circe, strange woman, wailed a chant as we approached: "I dreamed the walls of my house were foul with blood! Fire was licking at my magic drugs, but I quenched the fire with the blood!"

Medea and Jason knelt before her, covering their faces with their mantles, so I knelt too. She did not seem to notice me at all, and for that I was grateful. She was as beautiful as a young woman, but she was very old at the same time, and very frightening.

Circe suddenly changed into a puzzled, hospitable lady. Even as she motioned to her terrible creatures to get out of her way, she began to talk: "Now who are you, young man and young woman, who have come to visit poor lonely Circe on this island? Come into my house, come into my house. But your friends in the ship must come too, of course. Oh, we'll have feasting and music — we'll have a banquet, and I'll treat you very well."

Medea and Jason stood silent with their heads bowed until she repeated, "Come into my house." Then they walked with her, not looking up.

She invited them to sit in chairs, but they crouched instead in the cold ashes of the hearth, and Jason thrust the blade of his sword into the earth floor.

"Ah, you are suppliants," Circe said, no longer pretending not to know why they had come. "And you bring evil with you!" she screamed. "It is because of you that I dreamed of blood. There is blood guilt on you. Woe, woe to those who do evil!"

I tried to pretend I was not there, but when one of her terrible creatures — a gray cat with the face of an old man — rubbed against me, I choked back a cry. Orpheus' voice rose in the distance, and the old-man-cat padded out, attracted by the sound.

"You are murderers!" Circe growled. "But great Zeus, who hates killing, forgives killers if they seek asylum at my hearth."

She gave certain orders to her empty-faced maid servants, and one of them brought a suckling pig. Circe stabbed its throat with a bronze knife and let the blood run onto the outstretched hands of Jason and Medea while she screamed in a language I do not know.

Then she poured libations of wine and other liquids and called on Zeus the cleanser. The maid servants carried out the refuse while others built a fire so that Circe could burn oat cakes with prayers to Zeus.

"Their hands are lifted up to you, Great One," she cried. "Their hands are wet with blood. Forgive! Relent!"

Her mindless maidens chanted with her.

When the ceremony was finished, she took Medea's hand and said, in an entirely different voice, "Let me look into your eyes. Yes, my brother's child. And you killed your brother!"

Medea had not killed him, but she accepted Jason's guilt because it was fated.

The nymph Circe kept changing in frightening ways,

123

not in appearance but in attitude. One moment she coaxed and cooed. Then like lightning she flashed into rage: "Leave my house — leave my island — I will not give you shelter here!"

Medea knelt before her and asked softly, "Will my father's sister not give me refuge? And a promise that the Lord Jason will reach home safely?"

I shuddered, thinking that I would rather be dead than live among these deformed beasts.

"Leave my island!" Circe screamed. "Your fate is not here. Your fate is in a far country with your husband, who killed your brother. Ah, woe!"

Still kneeling, Medea said, "I have no husband."

"You will marry to save your life," Circe chanted. "You will live in a country far from Colchis. Sail away, sail away, for my brother's ships are following you!"

Jason was startled by that. He almost spoke, but then he shook his head, looking grim, and pulled his sword from the earth floor and bowed a courteous farewell to the powerful nymph, Circe.

Medea stood beside him and looked into his face, and they walked out side by side. I followed with Medea's drugs, which she would never need on Circe's island.

Medea walked with her mantle across her face, wailing a ritual chant of grief.

When *Argo* sailed from that dreadful island, Medea and Jason sat in the wooden pit, facing each other but not speaking, not looking. Their faces were covered by their mantles, and their shoulders were bowed in shame or grief.

124

I climbed to the little afterdeck where Orpheus sat staring across the water.

Circe was striding along the beach with the wind blowing her robe and her hair, wailing and weaving magic with her hands. She stopped and stared at *Argo*. Then she shrieked:

"Beware of Scylla and Charybdis! Beware the cliff and the whirlpool!"

She threw back her head and laughed like a madwoman. Her mindless maidens scampered around her, cackling with laughter.

I began to cry, because everything that had happened was so dreadful. Orpheus understood. He had watched those awful girls and had made music to keep the misshapen monsters away from us.

"It is told," he said quietly, "that the creatures of Circe are made of parts that were left over when men and animals were first formed. And there are other stories, that the nymph can change men into beasts. That is why our men did not leave the ship.

"Soon you can forget all these terrors, little Daphne. Now we are in waters that we know. We are on our way to our own homes, after we establish Jason as king in his land."

Remembering that Medea and I were never going home, I cried harder. He sang to me until my tears dried.

That night, on another island where we made camp, Medea said, "Daphne, I have one last hope. My father has a claim to the kingdom of Corinth, and therefore I have. But where is Corinth? And are we going there?"

"I will try to find out, my lady," I promised.

So I mentioned casually, to one man or another, "In Colchis we heard of a place called Corinth. Where is it?"

Someone would point — because now the Argonauts thought they knew where we were, although I didn't — but pointing did not tell me anything.

Orpheus said, "I know where it is from Peiria, but I have never been there. Butes the bee-master may know. He is from Attica."

Butes drew a map in the sand, but I did not know where Attica was.

Cepheus was from Arcadia, and he knew where Corinth was. He drew a map in the sand. But I did not know where Arcadia was.

Castor and Polydeuces knew where it was in relation to Sparta, but that did not help me either.

I was able to tell my lady that *Argo* would put in at Corinth if the wind were right, but only to replenish supplies.

Then one day we came to the Sirens' Isle.

People who have heard the story of the Argonauts say knowingly that one of the world's mysteries is what song the Sirens sang. I know what they sang to me, but no two of us could tell it the same way, because the song was different for each.

Before we really heard the alluring, melancholy music, we felt it as a terrible weariness and loss. The way was so long, and why did we keep trying? We could never go back. We had been to the end of the world, and still we traveled. The journey could end only in drowning, with our choked voices crying hopelessly as the dark sea sucked us down. *So why not now?*

That would be better than struggling any more. *So good, so good to rest down where the fishes are. Why not now?*

It was a deadly spell that slowed the blood and made the breath balk. The haunting voices said, *Give up, give up. You have no hope. You will never see your parents again or your brothers and sisters. Slide down into the welcoming water. Why not now?*

The rowers slowed their stroke and gazed across the sea toward the island, yearning for rest. The men drooped on the benches of *Argo*. Nothing mattered any more.

Medea's grasp on my arm relaxed, because nothing was worth while. The Sirens' song was a doom in the bones. All the effort of life was wasted. I began to cry, and Medea was weeping beside me — Hecate's priestess, who was trained to smile at terror. And Atalanta sobbed, she who had boasted that she did not cry out even from an arrow wound.

The story I have heard is that Jason was strong enough to resist and to shout for Orpheus to sing against the distant music. That is not true. Jason was as helpless as a baby.

Orpheus saved us. Roughly brushing tears from his eyes with a swipe of his brawny arm, he looked around, and I saw through my own tears that his face was twisted with grief and horror.

Orpheus could not endure the suffering of others. He

shuddered. Then, with great effort, he reached for his lyre. Half sobbing, he began to sing:

"A little more? Another stroke? Pull the oar. Just once more. That's all it takes. Just once more. And another. Then one more."

One of the rowers shouted something and tried to leap overboard, but another man seized him. A few of them collected themselves enough to pull their oars to the short beat — a little more, another stroke, just once more, that's all it takes. They moved as if in a nightmare, but they straightened the trailing oars in the rippling sea. All of them still stared toward the source of the far-off, baleful music.

Another rower shouted and leaped overboard before anyone could stop him. The men yelled, "Butes, Butes! Come back!"

But he swam with great strokes toward the Sirens' Isle — for a little while, only a little while. Then his strength failed and he sank.

The cries of the Argonauts changed to a dismal wail of mourning. Butes would never again tend his beehives in Attica.

Then Orpheus' voice boomed out:

"Home again, home again! You know where your homes are, men!"

He was stroking the lyre fast now, although we could not hear the gentle sound of its strings.

"Pull again, pull again, heroes homeward bound now! Another shore is ours, men. Past this place, past this place — pull, men, pull now!"

His glorious voice put heart into the men. The muscles of their arms moved like mice scurrying under the sun-darkened skin. *Argo* leaped through the water, and still Orpheus sang.

Sweat ran off the mighty, laboring shoulders of the lords and sons of kings, and *Argo* surged on — but the men still stared wistfully at the island as it dropped into the distance.

When we were too far away to hear the invitation to death, Orpheus leaned forward with his head on his arms, exhausted, and the rowers rested. They must have felt what I felt — that something lovely was lost forever. But it is better to live than to heed the Sirens' song.

The winds took us again, in spite of the Argonauts' skill with oars and sail. We all knew now that certain things were fated, and the prophets knew what some of them were.

We had a quiet landing that night on another island and a peaceful camp. Melampus and Mopsus watched flights of birds anxiously and addressed us after the evening meal.

Mopsus spoke first: "My brother prophet and I foresee great danger ahead. You heard the nymph Circe speak of Scylla and Charybdis, the cliff and the whirlpool. We will have to pass between those two if the gods will it."

The other prophet stood. "I have heard of Scylla and Charybdis. So have some of you. I heard they were two monsters, one that clutches men up and one that claws ships down."

The Argonauts moaned agreement.

"If *Argo* goes that way, she goes that way," Melam-

129

pus said. "No man is master of *Argo*. She is protected by her beam made of wood from Dodona, sacred to Zeus. We are protected by our own courage — and by the gods, if they love us."

A bronzed Argonaut stood to ask leave to speak, and Melampus held out the speaker's staff to give him permission. The man took it, and I saw that he was Peleus, the one who grieved for his lost sea-nymph wife, Thetis.

Peleus spoke briefly: "We must pass between the cliff and the whirlpool, and our danger will be very great. But we will have help from great powers. This is a promise. I cannot tell you more than this, because I have sworn I would not."

He gave back the staff and would not say any more.

Remembering what Orpheus had told me about Peleus' sorrow, I guessed that he had had a sign from his lost wife, Thetis, that she and her sister Nereids would help *Argo* through the perils ahead.

The next day Peleus was lookout. We heard him shout, "Land ho! Breakers! White water!"

Three men on the port side warned, all in one voice, "Fire from the sea!"

I was sitting in Peleus' usual rowing seat just then, so I saw these terrors. Ahead of us, far away, was a passage where two seas met — we had been expecting that. White breakers dashed far up on the rocks in pale fury. That was the cliff, and at the foot was the whirlpool.

Off to one side in the distance, the sea vomited fire, or else it came from an island that was hidden in the smoke and mist. We could see the flames and even hear the hiss as liquid rock struck the distant sea.

That was one of the workshops of the smith god Hae-phestus. We had heard about them. Where he works at his smithy under the sea, the flames from the forge burst up to the surface.

Orpheus began to sing a hymn to Haephestus, and there were no more eruptions of fire.

Jason ordered, "Ten men to reef the sail!" and the ten whose turn it was leaped from their benches and set to the hard task, working fast and skillfully.

Ancaeus the steersman asked doubtfully, "Is it any use to row?"

Jason yelled to Peleus, "Shall we row?"

Only Peleus knew what Peleus knew. He stood up and took command.

"Beyond the cliff and the whirlpool," he shouted, "are the Wandering Rocks. We must not row. We must sit still and give thanks to our powerful helpers. There is nothing else for us to do."

I hastened to clamber down to Medea, and we clutched each other and bales of freight to keep from being rolled into the water that sloshed under our platform.

Argo tossed and twisted and cried out in pain. She leaped toward the grim gray cliff that towered over us on one side. But something pulled her back from it, and she whirled around like a leaf in the vast whirlpool. Then some force freed her from that, and she charged toward the cliff again and was repelled.

Then we were in calm water, without a sail and with no oar power, but still we moved toward the Wandering

Rocks. When Medea loosed her grasp around me, there were bruises on my arms, and my lip was sore where I had bitten it.

Now that the noise of the furious water no longer beat in our ears, I could hear the gasps of the men on the rowers' seats. They were hanging over the sides as far as they dared, watching something we could not see.

Above, we could see towering rocks on both sides, but *Argo* raced through between them as they moved apart, and they did not clutch her.

Later, three different men told me in wonderment what they had seen as we made that perilous passage: white shapes among the waves, like a school of dolphins playing — the Lady Thetis and her sisters, guiding *Argo* to safety.

After that we had a quiet day or two, and then we came to an inhabited island. The Argonauts stood to their weapons and kept *Argo* afloat in shallow water while Jason conversed with some fishermen on the shore:

"What land is this?"

"The island of Corcyra, where great Alcinous is king. What ship is that, and what master?"

"The ship is *Argo*, blessed by Zeus. The rowers are lords and princes from far places in Greece, and Jason son of Aeson is master. We ask the king's permission to land here."

One man on shore went running with that message, and another asked, "What port do you hail from?"

"Many ports to which we won't return," Jason answered — rather crossly, because he was not accustomed

132

to answering so many questions from ordinary people.

"Do you hail from Aeetes' city in Colchis?" the fisherman insisted.

Jason yelled, "What makes you ask that?" and the man answered, "A Colchian ship has been here searching for *Argo* and a captured princess. It is somewhere out of sight but not far."

A groan went up from the Argonauts, and Medea gasped.

Someone up on the rowing benches barked some commands I had not heard before, in all our wanderings, and half the rowers jumped down into the wooden pit and went to work at heaving certain bales out of the way and hastily unroping certain others.

Castor spoke to Medea: "Will you and your handmaiden move, Princess? You're sitting on what I need. Here, I'll help you up to the benches. Even if they start shooting from the shore, you're protected by our shields. Down here you may get hurt."

We scrambled out of the way, with his strong help, and then we could see what the men were unpacking. It was their ceremonial garments, which they had not needed since that dreadful day we sailed from Colchis.

Medea clutched my hand as we watched. Their fine robes, dyed purple or red or deep blue, or of fine bleached white wool with colored borders, were carefully packed in wrappings of leather. The leather was cunningly worked and paper thin; it was treated somehow so as to be watertight, and then laced with leather cords.

133

"Their fine clothes are terribly wrinkled," I commented. "They should be hung in the wind to blow smooth."

There was in Medea's voice something like a strangled laugh. "But they can't hang them over the side of *Argo*," she replied. "That would look too much like the washing place where I used to oversee the serving women when they did the palace laundry."

The fine lords would just have to meet the local king with wrinkled clothing, then. I felt that it served them right.

"My lady, shall I get your fine white robe and your jewelry? And I must do my best with your hair." Orpheus had made me a brush from a piece of a bear's hide.

Medea was wearing her tattered brown robe, washed a few days before but really ragged.

She drew away and answered coolly, "Oh, no. I shall wear black, with my hair hidden by a black mantle, and no jewelry. We are captives, you know. We must walk humbly and let the great lords parley."

Atalanta came climbing along the bench row in her short, dirty dress with her hair in snarled braids. Once again, she was going to be out of place, neither a prince nor a lady.

"I suppose," she remarked in her usual challenging way, "that you're going to look as beautiful as the moon when we get to the palace? If we don't have to fight a battle, that is."

"I shall be in black," Medea replied, "as is proper for a captive far from home."

134

Atalanta burst out, "What shall I wear? I don't know what to do!"

Medea astonished her by answering, "I'm sure Daphne will be glad to help you with your hair. She has a brush, and it does need brushing. Won't you, Daphne?"

I gulped, "Yes, my lady," and Atalanta gulped, too.

We got down into the wooden pit, out of the wind, and when any of the men came near and wanted us to move, Atalanta snarled at them to stay out of the way. She kicked one in the shin with her heavy-soled sandal to enforce the command, and he yelped and then laughed.

My fingers to sort out the loose snarls and a bronze knife to cut out the tight knots and the brush to smooth the dark curls into waves worked wonders with her hair. Fortunately she had washed it a few days before. That was something she didn't do often enough.

"The trouble," I told her, "is that one braid will be shorter than the other because of that fire we went through. Shall I cut the other side to make it even? I can do it with the knife."

She was peering into her polished shield for a mirror, but it was tarnished from the weather, and she couldn't see herself very well. She shook her head.

"Wouldn't it be all right," she asked pathetically, "if I just let it hang loose, the way other girls do?"

I suddenly pitied her. She was uncertain about the things a girl should just know, but of course the poor thing had been brought up by rough shepherds.

"I could do it in a grand way," I said, "if we had some

135

pins. Make a big, soft twist back here, with curls on the sides, and a couple of loops, this way."

I knelt before her and looked into her face and saw that she was almost beautiful. Her skin was weathered, but so was Medea's, although not so much because I massaged her face with olive oil every chance I got. But poor Atalanta had seldom *wanted* to look beautiful, and now she was tense and anxious.

"Pins," she said. "I'll get you pins. Who will complain if I whittle a bit from my own rowing bench?"

She climbed up to it like a cat, pulling her knife out of its scabbard on the way, and came down very soon with a dozen thin wooden skewers.

"Those will do very well," I said. "But now the wind has you all mussed up again! You'd better put your ceremonial dress on before I do your hair."

Atalanta shouldered a couple of men out of her way, found her clothing bale, and brought out her dress — one that had been the gift of Medea's sister, since she had no good robe when she came to Colchis.

When I got through with her, she looked quite presentable.

"Drape the veil," I suggested, "to protect your hair from the wind but not to hide it all. And when it comes time to disembark, remember that you can't possibly do it without a strong man's hand to help you. Don't just vault over the side, the way you always do."

"I'll remember," she promised grimly. "Let's see, which one shall I tell to help me?"

"Don't tell anyone," I scolded. "Just stand there trembling and looking frail and let *them* get the idea. Now go sit down where the wind won't muss you up."

Medea came down then and changed to her plain black robe and mantle. I told her anything she might not have heard of my conversation with Atalanta, and she said with a hint of laughter in her voice, "But they're not accustomed to having Atalanta look frail. They might not notice. Drop a hint to three or four of the men — those she hasn't had any fights with lately."

I went up and spoke to Orpheus first; he was dressed and fine with his golden beard neatly trimmed. There were still loud "ouches" from down in the wooden pit as the Argonauts neatened their beards with their knives or had others do it, for lack of mirrors.

"Good idea," he agreed. "I'll pass the word to half a dozen of the men so that for once in her life the Lady Atalanta will know what it's like to be cherished. And," he added, smiling, "I'll set *you* down as if you were a rose petal. Ah, someone's coming!"

Peleus, below us, shouted, "Is it a festival or a fight?"

The ship's company was tense. If armed men were coming, the Argonauts could shuck off their ceremonial robes in an instant and seize their weapons.

There was a glitter among the trees — that was polished armor. There was a waving of colored banners. Then there was the great, welcome white one that meant "Come in peace," and beside it walked an old man carrying a herald's staff decked with white ribbons. That meant, "We will talk."

After him, came a regal gray-bearded man in a purple

robe, with a handsome woman beside him, and both wore circlets of gold on their heads.

A buzz went around *Argo*: "King Alcinous himself and his queen!"

Then a roar of welcome from the Argonauts rattled the banked shields. They snatched down the shields to show that we came in peace, too.

I glanced at Medea. Her face might have been carved from ice. She held her head high, and tears were trickling down her cheeks.

I squeezed her hand. "If we cannot stay here," I whispered, "maybe they will help us get to Corinth."

She did not answer.

The King's men ran out and pulled *Argo* close to shore. Our men went over the side like the athletes they were, disdaining the slanted landing stage that this port had. Atalanta couldn't even walk down the landing stage. She stood trembling at the top, looking helpless — although when she wore her battle armor she very much resembled statues of the goddess Athena.

Faithful to his promise, Orpheus had six of the tallest Argonauts hand her down, and she descended like the most delicate princess in the world. I was pleased to note that she had her robe draped so that it not only hung well but also covered her battle scars.

The six nobles escorted her to the King and Queen, and Orpheus came back up the platform for Medea. Jason should have done it, but as leader of the expedition he was conversing with the King.

Medea had her own plan for leaving the ship. She slipped past Orpheus like a shadow, evading his hand,

and ran down and dropped on her knees, a barefoot sup-
pliant, before the Queen and kissed the hem of the royal
robe.

This was so startling that Orpheus forgot about his
rose petal until I was almost past him. Then he picked
me up, smiling, and carried me down to be with my lady.

11

QUEEN ARETE drew the kneeling Medea to her feet and kissed her. Medea cried, "My lady, pity me! I disobeyed my father, and I must suffer for it."

Arete said, "There, there," as to an injured child, and Medea's self-control broke at last.

Then the Argonauts learned for the first time how terrible could be the anger of Medea. She paced among them, screaming, and they drew back before the golden fire in her eyes.

"You betrayed me," she screamed, "after I saved you! You are homeward bound with the golden fleece — and I am a homeless captive. I gave you back your homes! I gave you your lives! But I am a wanderer in foreign lands!"

Jason stepped forward and put his hand on her arm in a placating way, but she shook it off, crying, "My father's ship is in these waters, searching for me. Because of me, my brother is dead. Will you fight, or will you give me up to my father's mercy?"

The Argonauts looked at one another, embarrassed. Then, as one man, they raised their clenched fists and roared, "Defend her!"

Jason gave her a look of fury. It was plain to everyone that his captive did not trust him.

"Do you vow it?" Medea demanded, and the men shouted, "Yes!"

With the King and Queen looking on, they could hardly do otherwise! Of course a promise like that is not really binding unless one makes it sacred by calling on the gods, but the King would require them to keep it while they were in his country.

Medea should have stopped with that, but she was too distraught. She cried out in a strange language and paced and wove spells with her hands until the Queen said, "There, there," and tried to lead her away to the palace.

"No, Madame," Medea said. "I shall stay here while the men plan the defense."

The rest of them went up to the palace, except for a few who stayed to guard the ship in case the Colchians sailed into view. My lady sat for hours, a bowed, black-clad figure, under a tree.

She spoke only once: "Bring me the ivory box," she commanded. But she did not open it. She held it on her knees.

The lords and princes came back to the ship late from feasting at the palace and, seeing Medea under the tree in the moonlight, slunk by her as they unloaded their weapons and shields and sheepskin beds from *Argo* to spread them on the shore. Two of them did sentry duty, armed.

I awoke on the grass under the tree, aware of movement. A man was coming down the road from the palace. In the moonlight I could see that he held in his hand the herald's staff with white ribbons: He brought an official message.

"Lord Jason!" he intoned — and the Argonauts were instantly on their feet, awake, with their swords in their hands.

Jason stepped forward and laid down his sword ceremonially as a token of respect to the white ribbons. The herald recited:

"A message from the Queen, my lord. The King has made his decision. He does not want war with the great Aeetes of Colchis. If Princess Medea is a maiden, she must go back with the Colchian ship. But if Princess Medea is a wife, the King will not separate her from her husband. A messenger from the far side of the island says the Colchians will probably sail into this harbor in the morning!"

There was no more sleep that night for anyone. Suddenly the shore was alive with lights and noise and people. The Queen came bustling, surrounded by servants bringing the things required for a royal wedding.

"Ah, my dear, this is your wedding day," she cried happily.

Queen Arete herself dressed Medea in a white robe from the palace — "I wore it for my own wedding," she said.

Some ladies of the court — yawning and rumpled from sleep — took Medea away for the ceremonial bath. Some of Jason's friends led him off for the same purpose. But it all went so hurriedly that it didn't seem right. Medea seemed dazed. She simply did what she was told, with tears running down her cheeks.

Menservants came driving sheep, confused and baa-
ing, for the wedding sacrifice that was customary on this
island, and others brought wine for the libations.

The Queen gave orders to deck a certain sacred cave
for the bridal chamber. Dozens of girls came running
with their arms full of flowers, and others brought hastily-
made leafy garlands for both men and women to wear on
their heads.

Queen Arete remembered even me, the nobody from
a peasant's hut, Daphne the shadow of Medea. The
Queen did not know my name, or need to, but she saw
me in the shadows and said, "Here, child, I have something for you to do. You are closer to the bride in friendship than anyone else. You must do what her mother or
her sister would have done if she were in her own homeland. Your hands shall carry the marriage torch. Now
don't go away!"

She clapped her hands and gave orders to some more
servants. Go away? I was so overcome that I couldn't
even breathe.

The procession of lights was beautiful. The Queen's
ladies carried burning torches and sang as they followed
a winding path that led to the sacred cave of Macris,
where a nymph who had fed honey to the infant god Dionysus had once lived. The men carried torches (the
Argonauts carried their battle spears, too) and sang a different chant, with Orpheus' great voice leading them.

They lined up in front of the cave, and then I came,
carefully carrying a bigger torch (cunningly wound of
dried vines soaked in olive oil, so it was not heavy), and
lighted Jason and Medea into the flower-filled cave.

I left my torch there. When the procession started
down again, the sky was pink with dawn, and I was weeping. Medea's wedding should not have been like this!
But her life was saved.

As soon as the procession returned to the shore, it
broke up so that the Argonauts who had been guarding
the ship could take part in the merrymaking at the palace. The whole crowd — except some of the young
nobles of the island, who stayed on guard at the shore —
went singing and laughing up through the woods.

Young Meleager seized my hand and commanded,

"Come along, Daphne." Atalanta stalked beside us, frowning with jealousy. I managed to get lost from them at the palace, not wanting any arguments with that quick-tempered lady. Her hair was beginning to fall down.

The palace was very grand indeed.

The walls were covered with bronze trimmed with blue enamel, and the golden doors were held by silver posts. Beside the doors were statues of dogs made of gold and silver, and golden boys held burning torches. This was a very rich palace where people did not worry about war.

I wandered through a corridor and heard a baby cooing and a woman laughing. She was the nurse, and the baby was the royal princess, Nausicaa. We got along very well, in that quiet place away from all the noisy people.

"It is a long time," I said, "since I have played with a baby," so the nurse let me hold her.

It didn't stay quiet very long. Girls kept drifting in, the Queen's young servants, giggling and whispering to one another and asking silly questions. They weren't at all like Medea's maidens. They didn't know what I meant when I asked politely what their special talents were and what their education was like. They wanted to know about our adventures, they said — but when I tried to tell them, they only giggled. They were a mannerless lot. I was suddenly homesick.

A great shouting elsewhere in the palace startled us. I kissed the baby and gave her back to the nurse and ran to see what was happening. The girls ran after me, giggling.

A breathless messenger had arrived in the courtyard, after running from the other side of the island, to tell the King that the Colchian ship was on the way to our harbor and would come as soon as the wind permitted.

The Queen told King Alcinous, "Now is the time to tell those intruders what you decided last night — that you will not give up Medea."

"I shall certainly tell them," he agreed. "Nobles all! Take arms and prepare to fight on the shore!"

The Queen did not let the possibility of an impending battle interfere with the wedding celebration. Soon Medea and Jason were seated on chairs in the courtyard while servants paraded by with fine gifts. There were great clay jars of wine and metal mixing bowls and heaps of linens for the household that the bride would sometime supervise. There were rich robes and jewelry.

I seized the opportunity to collect something useful. I asked one of the higher servants for some common clay bowls and plates. He was courteous but puzzled until I explained, "*Argo* has come a long way and almost all our plain dishes have been broken. A tall silver pitcher is not very useful when what is needed is a cup to hold drinking water."

He nodded and sent a couple of girls scurrying for dishes.

"Fine lords don't think about such ordinary things," he agreed. "We'll have the dishes packed in straw."

There was no battle, after all. King Alcinous was very firm, once his wife had made up his mind for him. He told the Colchians that they would have to go back without Medea.

146

There was great activity around *Argo*, next time I went down to look. The Argonauts of course gave the King and Queen gifts of value equal to those received. This meant that almost the entire cargo had to be brought out and unpacked, and the new things had to be wrapped and stowed away. These things were of shapes and sizes different from the previous load. Although the gift-giving was only an exchange of valuable things, everyone concerned seemed to be pleased.

During those days on Corcyra I had not very much to do and too much time to think. I was sitting in the sand beside the sea crying softly when Orpheus found me.

"What is the trouble, little Daphne?" he asked, smiling.

"I was thinking of home," I said.

"But you didn't ask whether you could go home in the Colchian ship."

"No. I couldn't do that."

"Why not? Were you afraid?"

"I think my lady needs me."

"She will be Jason's queen," he said. "She won't be alone."

"But I am all she has from Colchis. Doesn't that matter?" Suddenly I was afraid that it did not, that I had thought myself important but was not important at all.

"It matters a great deal," Orpheus answered. "Sometime you will know how much it matters to the Lady Medea."

He stared across the water, not seeing it but looking at something in his thoughts.

"Sometime she will need your protection," he said.

That was so ridiculous that I almost laughed. "The wife of Jason will need the protection of a peasant's daughter? Lord Orpheus, you are kind but you are only trying to make me happy."

"Do you sometimes want to know the future?" he asked.

"Of course. But in Colchis it is not thought proper to inquire. Doesn't everyone want to know?"

"Everyone as young as you are wants to know. As we grow older, we are afraid to find out. But some of us are told. Mopsus knows what will happen to him. Let's find Mopsus and ask him what will happen to you."

We found the prophet sitting on a rock, looking across the sea as if he could not get enough of it, breathing deeply as if he loved to breathe and loved to live. Sometimes we forget what a privilege it is.

Orpheus said, "Medea's maiden is young enough to want to know her future."

Mopsus said, "She is very young. Girl, put your hands in mine."

I did, and he closed his eyes. When he released my hands, he said, "You will live where the world comes from both east and west. You will see ships pass that are not moved by either wind or oars, untouched by Poseidon."

I was too frightened to speak. To an island the world can come from any direction — but in what strange place could ships move without wind or rowers, untouched by the sea?

I ventured to ask, "Is it enchanted, then, and dangerous?"

"No more dangerous than any other place. You may find it enchanted, for you will be happy there. I don't know where it is. I've never been there.

"I am supposed to die from the sting of a serpent," he added. "In Libya. All that is necessary is for me never to go to Libya, then."

"We are not going there, are we?" I asked.

"Oh, no," Mopsus answered.

"Libya is far to the south, across a great sea," Orpheus explained. "We have no reason for going there. We are on our way home now, if the gods are willing."

On the seventh day after our arrival at Corcyra, we made ready to sail. At the last minute, the Queen came down to the shore, surrounded by those giggling girls, all carrying bundles.

"Medea, my dear," she said, very pleased with herself, "I have brought you one more wedding gift. In your new home, you will need maidservants. These are trained in certain skills, and they will serve you well."

The Argonauts gasped, but Medea retained her composure and thanked the Queen regally. To have refused the gift would have been a deadly insult.

Queen Arete was wonderfully kind — but where did she think we could find space for twelve more passengers?

12

THE ARGONAUTS were in good spirits when we left Corcyra, in spite of the extra passengers.

There was a good wind from the north, and the sail was up.

Orpheus began to make up a song, and as he finished each verse, everybody joined in: "Going home! Going home!"

Even the twelve girls sang it — a silly lot they were, because they certainly weren't going home. The Queen must have told them a fine story about the romantic adventures they would have in Medea's household. They were restless and curious, talking and giggling among themselves.

They did not know how they were supposed to act toward me, and I didn't know either. My situation was changed. I thought I should stay away from my lady so that she could talk privately with Jason if she wanted to do so. But there was little chance for conversation, because the wind blew our words or the banging of the leather sail drowned them.

I was trying to move forward in the ship to sit with Lynceus the lookout when one of the girls tripped me.

Then another one tried it. I glared and pointed my finger at her and recited some nonsense that we used for counting out in children's games back home. The girl cringed and shivered, assuming that I was putting a spell on her, and after that they were polite, when they remembered.

Lynceus frowned and remarked, "I don't like the looks of the weather. But surely the gods will be good to us now that we are so near our harbor! Only a few days more, you know."

"And where will we be when we get there?" I asked. Corinth did not matter any more. My lady would not seek refuge there. She was Jason's wife, and where he went, she would go.

"Why," answered Lynceus, "we will be on the beach of Pagasae Harbor within sight of Iolcus, Jason's city."

I didn't ask where that was.

Squinting at the sky, he began to chuckle. "I can't forget Queen Arete — wonderful woman. The King is not very decisive, you may have noticed. He only thinks he makes the decisions, because she convinces him that he did. I can just imagine what went on in the royal bedchamber after we arrived on the island.

"He was sleepy — he's much older than she is, you know. But she would not let him rest, because any delay would have been fatal to us. I'm sure she talked and talked and kept him awake until he groaned and turned over and said, 'All right, my dear, all right.'

"Then she said, 'That's what you've decided then?' And he agreed that it was, not knowing what it was — anything to get a little sleep.

"As soon as he was snoring, she leaped up and began waking the servants and issuing orders for the marriage ceremony — because that was what the king had decided should be done!"

He stopped laughing and scowled around at the sky. "We're going to have a bad storm — a gale from the north."

He yelled to warn the other men, but they didn't believe him.

Lynceus remarked, "I see land over to the left, but nobody else can, so far. That's the west coast of Pelops' Land. We'll go south around the end of it and then north, up the other side."

The wind suddenly hit us with a whistle, and the other Argonauts decided that his storm warning had been sound. Some of them leaped down to pack the cargo tighter, and others took down the sail and rolled it up. Then we were really crowded!

The whistle grew to a scream, and I climbed down and stumbled to the place where my lady sat. The girls from Corcyra didn't have wits enough to try to shelter her from the wind. They had stopped giggling. Half of them were white with fear, and the rest were green with seasickness.

Medea said, "Never mind, my dear. I wish we could do something for those poor girls. Bring them to me if you can. Perhaps I can take their minds off their fears. Tell them I can." She showed me the little golden ball on its chain.

Just stumbling to get near her took their minds off fear for a while. I promised them that the Lady Medea would

152

make them feel better. They huddled near her and stared at the twisting bright ball and into her eyes, and the sound of the wind was monotonous, so that they became calm.

"You are at home, doing your usual work," she told them. "Tell me what you are doing."

One by one, they told her of their skills. They were cloth dyers, cooks, gardeners, potters; they ground grain and cared for poultry and lambs and little pigs. She praised them, and they were pleased.

These, I understood, were not like Medea's maidens in Colchis, trained in manners and fine weaving and history and music. These were bond maidens, and they would be useful in her household — if the ship lived through the storm so that she could ever have a household.

She told them to sleep, and they cuddled up and slept. She put her arm around me and said, "They will be useful."

We had to go east, all the men kept saying, and they began to worry about it, for we were not going that way.

Calais and Zetes implored their father, the North Wind, to free *Argo*. They shouted to the sky that the men were going to row eastward and they hoped Boreas, the North Wind, did not object.

The rowers on the right began to pull the oars cautiously to a slow beat while the men on the left held their oars steady in the water. The wind blew harder than ever.

Huddled with Medea, one of the girls whimpered, "Why do they want to go east?"

"That is the way to the harbor of Pagasae," she explained. "My husband told me. We must go around the southern end of Pelops' Land and then north to Jason's kingdom."

The wind struck *Argo* broadside with a vicious slap while the rowers were turning her. The ship almost tipped over. We were all soaked with spray and sea water by the time she righted again. Two men hovered over the caldron with the precious fire in it, protecting it with a big piece of leather.

Some of them rigged a sea anchor to drag, to slow our progress, but aside from that we were at the wind's mercy.

The North Wind blew, and still we drove south, with no land in sight. Sometimes the wind played with us. I lost track of the days, but later the men said nine of them passed while the storm continued.

We were numb with misery and fear. It was a dismal fear that became worse as we went ever farther from Pelops' Land.

We had felt melancholy when we passed the Sirens' Isle; we had yearned to leap into the sea and be done with our troubles. Now we suffered a different melancholy. It sapped our strength.

Even Lynceus the lookout was too weary to watch, and when he yelled "Breakers ahead!" it was too late.

Jason yelled orders, and the men straightened on their rowing benches, but they could not slow the ship.

"No use — up oars!" groaned Jason. A great wave swept *Argo*, dashing her against a rocky shore. Some of the rowers tumbled down into the wooden pit. All Medea's girls screamed, including me — and so did Atalanta, who liked to boast that she wasn't afraid of anything.

Then *Argo* was in calm water, tangled in seaweed, lost in mist. The men were yelling: "*Argo*'s aground! . . . See if she's damaged. . . . Probably ripped the bottom out. . . . No, she's not taking in water. . . . Where are we?"

Mopsus the prophet said quietly, "This must be Libya."

The helmsman roared in anger, "Let someone else try to take her home. I can't."

The mist was so thick that nobody dared to leave the ship for a while, but as the sun burned it away we could see. Shallow water and sand. Nothing else.

The girls from Corcyra sobbed and wailed. We were all too discouraged to be thankful that the storm had stopped. Even Orpheus drooped on his rowing bench.

With great effort we disembarked and waded to shore. One of the men groaned, "The gods never meant for us to reach home," and sat down with his head bowed, hopeless and lost.

No one cared to eat. Most of our supplies were spoiled by salt water anyway. As darkness increased, we wrapped ourselves in our cloaks and lay on the sand, and the girls kept wailing until I began to cry too. That was a haunted shore.

In the morning Jason set grimly out to see whether any people lived nearby. He returned with staring eyes and open mouth. I thought he must have a fever, but he said he had seen a wonder and was shaken by it.

"Nymphs!" he gasped. "I saw nymphs. And they

commanded, 'Repay your mother.' Then they vanished."

Someone muttered, "What does that mean? He must be sun-struck."

Peleus sighed, "Who is our mother?"

"*Argo*? Yes they must mean *Argo*," Orpheus suggested. "But how to repay her?"

We were in a salty lake. Boreas had brought us into it, and we could not pass back over that rocky ledge.

We were disconsolate, not understanding why we should be punished this way or how to obey the command that Jason said the nymphs had given him.

Medea took me to one side and asked, "You have had no foreseeing about this?"

"No, my lady. My head swims with the heat. It is no use to hope for a foreseeing. They come uninvited."

"I wonder," she mused, "whether the dream game would help us. If you were to go into a dream, you might see."

I nodded, and she drew out the little golden ball.

"You are a cloud in the summer sky," she said. But I was not, I was only Daphne, feverish and thirsty.

"I do want to see my mother," I said.

Medea murmured, over and over, "Repay your mother. Now you are repaying your mother," and I went into a dream.

When she brought me out of it, I said, "I did not see my mother," and began to cry. "I was only pushing with my shoulder against a wall of wood."

"Was it a door you tried to open?"

"No. It moved, but it was not a door."

"Were you alone?"

156

"No. Others were there. A man was ahead of me, pushing the wall. Sweat ran down his back."

"Who was he?"

"I did not see his face."

I remembered something else: "The wall was rough, and I tasted salt."

"Wood and salt," Medea said thoughtfully.

She called Jason and Orpheus and Mopsus, because those two had prophetic powers, and told them what had happened.

"Wood and salt," Jason repeated. "That may be *Argo*."

Orpheus agreed. "She has been a good mother to us. How shall we repay her?"

"She carried us here," Mopsus interpreted. "Now we must carry her. With our shoulders, as Daphne saw in her dream, pushing her across the sand."

Jason slid his foot along the sand. "Yes, it moves easily — but will the ship slide on it?"

He gathered the company and explained the meaning of the nymphs' command.

"Let us try to push the ship with our shoulders against the planks," he urged. "*Argo* has carried us. Now help *Argo* get home."

The talking beam moaned. Perhaps the heat affected the wet timbers — or perhaps the ship spoke.

"Which way?" several men muttered. "Which way to go?"

Peleus implored the sky: "Give us a sign!"

The sign came. A horse came galloping along that desolate desert and tossed its golden mane in fright, turned sharply and galloped off. We heard it whinny.

We all cried, "That way! That way!"

We did not unload the ship but pulled it up on shore and pointed it in the direction the horse had gone.

We all pushed the ship, women as well as men. *Argo* went willingly. But when even one person stumbled and stepped aside, the rest could not budge her.

The sun beat down, and all of us were thirsty. There were only two clay jars of water left. In the storm, the seals on the others had been broken, and the sweet water was spilled or spoiled with salt from the sea.

Thirsty and exhausted, some of us began to see things that were not there at all, as one may when suffering from

a fever. I saw the clay pitcher that stood by the hearth in my father's hut, with water dripping from the sides — the very pitcher, with a piece broken out of the lip. Tears ran down my cheeks as water ran down that pitcher.

When we stopped to catch our breath, Orpheus implored, "Nymphs, queens, and powers, save us! Lead us to a gushing spring. . . . See them? See the nymphs?"

No one else saw them, but sharp-eyed Lynceus said, "Grass ahead — and three green trees!"

Some of the men broke away and began to run, but Jason roared them back.

"We take *Argo* where we go!" he said.

We did, slowly and painfully, one step at a time. There *were* three trees, and there *was* a spring gushing from a rock. We swarmed toward it like ants, but before we drank Orpheus commanded, "Wait."

He carried a bowl of water to *Argo* and poured it on the beam made from the sacred oak at Dodona, and a strange sound came from the wood. *Then* we drank.

Lynceus squinted into the distance. "I think the sea is not far away," he reported.

We were content to rest a while and fill the water jars and wash the sweat and sand off ourselves. Several of the men set out to explore, because we were now in a region of low hills.

After a while we heard a shout, and Atalanta said, "That is Canthus' voice."

He yelled, "Sheep! I found sheep!"

We saw the stupid faces of some sheep on a sandy ridge, and then Canthus' face, shining with sweat and triumph.

But just as he came into full view, he groaned and fell.

Half a dozen Argonauts seized weapons and ran toward him. When they returned, grim and silent, two of them carried his lifeless body. The others drove the sheep.

Jason said briefly, "The shepherd who killed him will sling no more stones."

We women set up a mourning wail, and the men began grimly to dig a grave. Mopsus was one of the diggers. He had spoken very little since — I remembered it with a shiver — he had said, "This must be Libya."

Now he stepped back from the grave to wipe sweat from his face, and we heard him cry out in a strangled voice, "A snake! A snake! I am bitten!"

Medea said sharply, "Daphne, bring the ivory box."

The box was on the sand; Medea had been carrying it in a sling made from her mantle, even while she helped move *Argo*. I seized it and ran after her.

"Don't look!" she warned me, but I couldn't avoid it. She was dangling the little golden ball before his eyes and soothing him with a spell as his body arched in a convulsion.

That kind of serpent is so venomous that no medicine can counteract its poison, but Mopsus died without pain. The snake he stepped on had bitten his heel, and his leg swelled enormously.

So the Argonauts dug the grave big enough for two men and heaped a great barrow of sand over it and marched around it three times in full armor. They sacrificed a sheep to Those Below, asking kindness for Canthus and Mopsus.

Then we went on, helping *Argo* to go home.

We launched her at last, more crowded than ever, in spite of leaving two of our company buried in Libya.

Now we had six struggling sheep with their feet tied together, lying among the baggage and blatting until we thought we would go mad. We needed the sheep, because our food supply was low, and nobody knew how far we still had to go.

Argo could not leave that unhappy shore. The harbor was like glass, but as soon as the rowers brought her into the open sea, the wind balked us again.

Even with the rowers pulling strongly, the ship could not move north. The girls from Corcyra began to wail.

Orpheus stood up in his place and shouted, "The gods in this land must require — " but the shrill wind and the girls' wailing drowned his voice.

He lost his temper. He glared at Medea and yelled, "Lady, keep those empty-headed women quiet!"

She nodded assent and held the ivory box high as a threat. The girls understood that it was full of wonders, good and bad. They quieted at once and sat with their mouths open.

Orpheus spoke again: "I think we must pacify the gods of this land, Libya, whoever they may be. We should leave them a sacrifice."

Two of the girls screamed. Perhaps human sacrifice is customary in their country — I have heard that it is in some places. But Medea simply looked at them, and they became quiet.

The men pulled *Argo* on shore again and dug into the baggage until they found and unwrapped a tall tripod

161

made of bronze. With proper respect they stood it on the sandy beach. They marched around it, singing religious songs and clashing their swords on their shields. A wave washed up and claimed the offering.

Then Argo sailed north — but toward what land?

Something moved and guided us. With the sail up, the sea glittering, the wind from the west, and only a little help from the oars, *Argo* sailed smoothly for two nights and a day. The sheep never stopped blatting. We landed on a fertile shore, but there were no people, no farms in sight.

Jason and a few of the other men held council to decide where we were. On a great piece of pale leather they had kept a record of the journey, with lines drawn in the directions we had gone, judging by the stars, and pictures as reminders of what had happened in various places.

The shore we had come to was unknown to any of us, like Libya and all those rivers where we had been lost. But some of the men had heard of an island called Crete, and they thought this was it.

"We are far from home," I heard Peleus say with a sigh, "but if this is Crete, we should go northwest."

We stayed two days and feasted on the sheep from Libya and dried some of the meat in strips in the fire smoke. The men wandered far, searching for farms, but that was wild country. We were hungry for bread and fruit. Two of the men brought back a basket of grain, not explaining how they got it.

Having no milling stones, we could not make flour

or meal, but the Corcyran girls boiled the grain with herbs and mutton for a satisfying stew.

There was no wine left in *Argo*'s jars. Some had been spoiled when their seals broke during the long storm and sea water got in. The rest had been used for libations to the gods of Libya and the spirits of Mopsus and Canthus.

We set out northwest from Crete, with the Argonauts hopeful about reaching their homes at last but worried because they were not sure where Pelops' Land was.

That night, with *Argo* moving swiftly before the wind across the moonlit sea, we were suddenly enveloped by blackness. The moon was swallowed up, and all the stars. There was no gleam anywhere, no sparkle on the water.

"I have heard of this," one of the men groaned. "It is the Pall of Doom on the Cretan Sea."

Jason asked, "Has any ship escaped it?"

Medea replied, "Someone must have escaped. How else would anyone know the name of it?"

They decided to pray for light, imploring Apollo, who is Helios, the lord of light. Orpheus sang to him, with the ship's company joining in the chorus. They were still singing when Linceus shouted, "Light! Dawn is coming!"

We did not know the name of the island where we beached *Argo*, but the name did not matter. We ate sparingly, for very little food was left. We offered thanks to Apollo, but there was no wine for the libation, so we used pure water instead.

The Corcyran girls, relieved to be safe again, became as silly as a yard full of poultry when a hawk flies over.

They gabbled and giggled at the idea of offering plain water, no matter how solemn the ceremony or how deep our thanksgiving. They laughed aloud and, growing too bold, made fun of the lords and princes.

This embarrassed the Argonauts and angered Medea. Some of the girls were laughing so hard that they rolled on the ground.

Medea screamed, "Stop that!" because screaming was the only way to get their attention. Sullenly they stared at her.

"I shall not punish you with a spell," she said. "But if you are rude once more, the ship will sail without you."

A few days later we came to another island — Aegena, the men agreed jubilantly. Now they knew where we were. Now they knew how to get home.

From there we sailed again, and one of the rowers shouted, "The coast of Attica! Athens is right over there! Alas, Butes will never see Attica again."

Then through a passage, and on our right, they said, was Euboea. Canthus would not return there.

"There's Aulis!" they cried.

Jason told Medea triumphantly, "Now we are almost home!"

She replied quietly, "Yes, my lord." Colchis was far away. Now her home would be where Jason was king.

13

When we neared the harbor of Pagasae, on the shore of Iolcus, Jason became very busy with orders — take down the sail, head for the shallow place at the left, easy now! The Argonauts had been there before — that was the place they had sailed from — and they had made so many landings that they did not need commands. *Argo* could have found her own good landing place with no help from anybody, for that matter.

The sail was rolled up in the wooden pit when we came into Pagasae, but the mast still stood, and on it, high up so that it could be seen from a distance, was fastened the golden fleece. The Argonauts looked at it with admiration and pride, but to me it was only an old sheepskin, very big and very dirty and the cause of all our troubles.

Jason told Medea proudly, "When I show that to old Pelias, he won't believe it. He thought I could not get the golden fleece. But now he will have to make good his promise and turn my kingdom back to me."

Medea looked at him with big eyes and answered, "Yes, my lord."

It happened that Atalanta heard Jason boast, and she was a great one for putting other people in their places.

although she was a great boaster herself. She spoke up rudely:

"Listen, Jason, do you think this is going to be easy? Is this old king going to hand over his staff of office to you without even an argument?"

It was wrong of her, of course, to embarrass him in front of Medea, but Atalanta never thought twice before she spoke, and she was always indignant or hurt when anyone showed offense.

Jason replied haughtily, "I do not trust King Pelias, of course. If we have to fight him, you need not take part in the battle, Lady Atalanta."

Then she was furious, naturally. "I'll be there!" she promised.

Orpheus, trying to bring peace, as he usually did, remarked, "There was a madness on us when we sailed from this harbor. We are older now, and wiser — and some of us are dead."

Atalanta gave him a suspicious glare, but she did not say anything more. She had got her point across: Our approach to the palace should be planned with caution.

Four small boats were in the harbor when we rounded the cape. The fishermen in them, seeing our ship, rowed for shore in great haste, pulled up their boats and ran — all but one man, who did not see the *Argo* in time.

Euphemus roared, "Come here, you!" and dived overboard. He was a very fast swimmer, and he caught up with the fisherman and, laughing, snatched one of the oars and tossed it aside. He began to tow the boat to shore, swimming with one arm, but the fisherman tried to hit

166

him with the other oar, so Euphemus roared and snatched that one away, too, and let it float.

When our men had pulled *Argo* into shallow water, Euphemus brought the trembling old fisherman to Jason. Others of our company stood guard on the shore, because the fishermen who had escaped would carry news of our landing to the city.

Medea went to stand near Jason, and I with her.

"Who rules this land of Iolcus?" Jason demanded.

"The King is Pelias, sir."

"What has become of the rightful ruler, Aeson?"

"I heard that King Pelias killed him, Lord, and his wife killed herself in grief. May I go now, Lord?"

"Not yet," Jason said, scowling. "Have you heard of a prince named Jason, the lost son of Aeson, who was reared by the Centaurs?"

"No, sir. I'm only a poor fisherman. What have I to do with the mighty?"

"What do you know of Pelias? Do his people like him?"

The old man was frightened, but he was too wise to take sides against the king — or for him, either. He said, "All I know is that he is an old man with three daughters."

Medea spoke then, with the majesty and kindness of a great queen.

"Old sir," she said, "you are chosen to have a great honor. And here is something to help you remember what I am going to tell you." She stripped a gold bracelet from her arm, and the old man almost fainted when she pressed it into his hand.

"You have heard of the goddess Hecate, no doubt," she said. The man's mouth opened in awe. "I am her priestess. Tonight we will celebrate a festival of the Dark One, the ceremony of rebirth, the Mystery of Life Renewed. Tell all the people."

"Yes, lady," he gasped.

"This is not an invitation," she said. "It is a command."

The old man trembled.

"Anyone who can come but does not come will insult the goddess. What you will see is an aged ram becoming a young, skipping lamb. Tell them in the city to bring the oldest ram in all the flocks — and music must come with him in honor of Hecate. Go now!"

She gestured toward the city, and the old man fled, limping.

She turned to Jason. "What the people will see," she promised, "will frighten the old usurper so much that he will not dare to refuse anything you ask. Now to prepare for the ceremony. Please unload the great bronze caldron."

She planned aloud: A shield where the firelight would shine on it as it turned, and someone to beat a booming drum — wood for the fire — where to let the people stand watching. She planned, and Jason gave the orders.

The last one was: "Bring back a small, skipping lamb — but don't let anyone see it."

A dozen of the Argonauts set out to steal a lamb — and brought back ten of them before long, but Medea kept only the smallest.

The sun had set and darkness was falling when we

168

heard music far off — pipes and flutes and horns and
drums. The procession was coming from the city.

A man in a white robe was leading an ancient ram that
had garlands twined on his curving horns. The ram stumbled, and the procession stopped. After a delay, someone brought a litter and four men carried the poor old
beast.

Medea glided fearlessly toward the people. She was
dressed in black. So was I. I walked behind her, terrified, but trusting in her power and wisdom.

She spoke to the panting old ram in a clear, sweet
voice: "Ancient one, sick and ready to die, you shall be
young again! The Dark Goddess will renew your youth
as a promise that all her people will live again." She cried
wildly, "Death is not forever! That is the promise of
Hecate, the Moon. The Moon wanes and dies — but the
Moon is born anew!"

A moan of fear and wonder went up from the people, and the Argonauts began a chant, led by Orpheus. The drum began to boom. The fire on the beach blazed up, and as we turned to walk beside the ram on its litter I saw the glitter of the shield twisting in the firelight.

Medea began a shrill chant.

I knew what was going to happen, because I had seen it before, but the others had not. The shield twisted in the firelight, and the great drum boomed. Medea paced and circled, chanting monotonously. She led the old ram to the fire and with the help of Castor and Polydeuces thrust it into the great caldron.

The people of the city were entranced and frightened. They sang the chorus as Medea chanted, and they swayed back and forth to the slow booming of the drum.

"You believe!" shrieked Medea.

"We believe!" moaned the people.

"Death is not forever!" she promised.

They answered, "Death is not forever!"

Suddenly a frisky little lamb leaped out of the caldron and danced away into the shadows.

"Great is Hecate!" Medea cried.

And they howled, "Great is Hecate!"

Then, with a great spitting of water on burning wood, someone overturned the caldron onto the fire, and the night was dark — except that the new moon was rising.

After the crowd had gone back to the city, the ship's company was strangely quiet, impressed by the ceremony.

Jason said in a low voice, "If old Pelias asks to be renewed, can you do it?"

"No, my lord. This is symbolic of youth renewed. I

can only perform this necessary ceremony in worship of the goddess, Hecate. I cannot renew the youth of an old man."

One of the Argonauts remarked, "But with this proof of your lady's power, Jason, the city is as good as yours now, without any battle. We'll be going home soon, to our own places. I wonder how everything is in my house, in my kingdom."

Someone else said, "Our prophets are dead, Idmon in Asia, killed by a wild boar, Mopsus in Libya, stung by a serpent. Orpheus, can you see our homes?"

"No," he answered. "Can Daphne farsee?"

"I will try, Lord Orpheus," I promised. "If I can touch your hands."

Meleager brought a cloth to blindfold me, and one by one the Argonauts held out their strong, calloused right hands for me to take between my hands.

The farseeing was sometimes clear and sometimes confused with foreseeing, but I told them what I could:

"Your people will welcome you. . . . The enemy is at your city gates. Creep in by darkness. . . . Peace and prosperity. Sheep grazing on the lush grass. . . ."

Medea urged me to go on.

"A grave and a young woman mourning . . . A little boy at practice with a sword. . . . An old woman weeps. An old man comforts her. . . . Your people need you.

"Blood — oh, blood and hatred among kinfolk! A burning brand snatched from the fire." Long later, I knew that this was Meleager's hand.

Medea said, "The girl is exhausted. We must not ask her any more."

But her hand was in mine, and I gulped as I said, "Smoke and flame, and a chariot drawn by — strange beasts of some kind."

There was a kind of scuffling, and one more hand came into mine.

"A father who is proud to claim his child," I said — and heard Atalanta gasp. "A foot race lost by one who has never lost before."

I pulled away, shuddering. This foreseeing frightened me more than the others. Something terrible was going to happen to Atalanta sometime.

Next morning the Argonauts argued about what they should do. I think they woke up arguing. They were making a great racket when I went to tell the girls from Corcyra to prepare whatever they could find for our first meal of the day. Seven of them were missing. The others knew where they were but would not tell. I ran to Medea.

"Only five girls are left," I said. "Do you suppose the others are looking for farms that might have food to spare?"

"I think they found their farms last night," she answered dryly, "or perhaps they found farmers."

They had been huddled in a terrified group after the ceremony, clacking like poultry when a hawk flies over. So now we had only five to worry about.

Medea said, "The Argonauts are in a hurry to go home."

We could hear them squabbling. What was the best way for Jason to confront old King Pelias and prove he had finished his quest and take over the kingdom?

"Tell me what they are saying," Medea commanded.

172

The men did not notice when I walked near enough to hear the arguments.

They wanted to unload *Argo* and divide the treasure then and there. They wanted to be all ready to leave before the day was over. Some would buy — or, more likely, simply take — pack animals and start overland. Others squabbled about whether ships might be expected to come into this harbor or what other port was the best one to go to.

Several of them actually went on board *Argo* and began to toss out their bales and boxes.

While the rest were still planning their strategy for approaching the city and the old King, a woman came screaming down to the shore.

"The King is dead!" she shrieked. "King Pelias is dead! Woe, woe!"

She was frantic with horror. Medea put a hand on her arm and said, "Be quiet."

The woman sobbed out what had happened:

"His own daughters killed him. They wanted to make him young again instead of old and sick like the ram. But when they stabbed him as the witch stabbed the ram at the caldron, he bled and gasped and died!"

Then she saw whose hand was on her arm and twitched it away, screaming, "Your fault! The foreign witch — your fault the King is dead!"

She fled screaming along the shore.

"Now we will have to fight the whole city," Jason groaned, "before I can claim my kingdom. And I have yet to mourn my parents and pour libations on their graves."

173

A roar of anger and disagreement went up from his companions.

"No more fighting!" one of them shouted. Others cried, "Home! Home!"

They launched *Argo* just as the army of Iolcus came streaming down the hill.

Only two of the girls from Corcyra were with us when we sailed from the harbor of Pagasae.

A story that I still hear sometimes is that Medea bewitched the daughters of Pelias, promising that they could make him young again if they killed him and bathed him in certain magic water with herbs in it. That is just another lie told about unhappy Medea.

The daughters of Pelias killed him. Medea had nothing to do with it. The strange thing is that the same people who tell the lying tale about how Medea plotted the death of Pelias praise her, in a way, for doing it. He deserved it, they say, for he killed Jason's parents. Medea helped Jason get revenge, they say.

That is not true. When we came to Iolcus and left again, Medea had not yet suffered enough to want vengeance on anyone for anything. She knew grief and she felt guilt for her brother's death, which she could not prevent, but it was later that she learned bitterness that turned into hatred.

When we were in *Argo* with the army clamoring and shooting arrows from the beach, I dared to ask my lady, "Where are we going?"

"To Corinth," she replied, "and Jason shall rule my kingdom."

14

THE NIGHT before we reached Corinth, we beached the ship at an island, and the Argonauts held council.

"I am going to sleep," Medea told me. "You may sleep too."

"But how will you claim your city?" I asked. "If it is a strong place, the Argonauts can't simply conquer it — and anyway they are all anxious to go home."

She patted my arm and laughed lightly. "We'll let them argue about that," she replied, "and after they decide something impossible, I'll tell them what we are really going to do."

Dawn was breaking when Jason came to where we slept. He was disconsolate and angry.

"They have given up," he reported. "They say it is no use. If we attack the city, we'll all be killed. So they are simply going to their own homes. They don't care what happens to us." He sat on the sand with his head bowed. "I don't know what to do."

"My lord, let me suggest something," Medea told him meekly. "Daphne, you may leave us while I confer with my husband."

So I left them and found that the other two Corcyran

girls had run off during the night to the village on this island. That was good riddance.

We sailed when daylight came and beached *Argo* a good distance from Corinth. Half a dozen of the Argonauts went into the city to find out what the situation was there. Meanwhile the rest unloaded the ship, because the kings and princes were determined to make their way to their own kingdoms even if they had to leave some of their treasure behind and face unknown perils as solitary travelers.

When the spies came back there was another council, with Medea taking part. Then she told me we were going into the port.

"Your plan is mad!" Jason fretted.

"What better one is there?" Medea asked reasonably. "The King here is newly dead. Now is the time."

Jason and five of the others were the men in the party that walked into the city, and Medea asked me to accompany her because a queen should have at least one attendant. The men wore their swords and short daggers but did not wear armor because they did not want to attract attention.

The port of Corinth was the noisiest place I had ever been in. I had not dreamed there was such a busy place in the whole world. Men were loading ships and unloading others with big cranes that squealed hideously as they moved. Men were carrying loads on their shoulders or beating donkeys that carried loads or repairing ships or building ships or yelling about something. There was pounding and slamming and banging and sawing everywhere.

Medea wore black, with a veil completely covering her face. We stopped at a small bower made of dried brush where a sweating man was handing out food to other sweating, dirty men — some of them black men with kinky black hair — who crowded in to receive it.

A richly dressed, scowling fellow with a great black beard, resplendent in a robe of blue and yellow, stood by with a whip in his hand to keep them in line. He was a ship's captain, seeing that his crew was fed. And well fed, too — over a charcoal fire meat was sizzling, and it smelled very good. It looked like something we had at home once or twice a year on feast days, sheep's intestines stuffed with chopped meat and vegetables and roasted over coals. In Corinth, even slaves ate well!

Jason spoke politely to the black-bearded man: "Sir, do you understand my language?"

The man glared as he answered, "Certainly. Did you think I'm a foreigner?"

"I think," said Jason, "that you are a prosperous Corinthian, influential in the port and the city."

"You're right," the man answered, mollified. "Stay out of there, you scavenging dog!" he yelled at a man who tried to get into the food line. Then, to Jason, "Well, sir, what do you want?"

"To give the city its rightful ruler," Jason told him.

"A fine time for it," the man answered. "The one we had just died, leaving no family."

"I share your grief," Jason said courteously.

"Nobody's grieving." He cracked his whip. "Out, you dog!"

"The rightful king is Aeetes," Jason purred.

"He sailed away when I was too young to care," the merchant said. "For a stranger, you know a lot. Most strangers don't care what our government is as long as they can get in, get rich, and get out."

"The daughter of Aeetes is wise beyond understanding. She is skilled in magic. She can farsee and foresee."

"Didn't know he had a daughter," the man grumbled. He stepped forward and cracked his whip at two men who were having a fight.

"You know, I suppose," said Jason, "that the children of Helios have golden eyes?"

"I know that. Never met any of them. But Aeetes had those eyes, I've heard."

Jason turned to Medea. She pulled back her veil and said to the man, "Look into my eyes."

I had my fist clenched under my mantle, for at this moment we could all be killed. The black-bearded man stared at my lady with his mouth open.

"I have come to claim my father's kingdom," Medea said, "and to give you a good ruler. I am Medea, daughter of Aeetes. This is my husband Jason, son of Aeson."

"By Zeus, I think I believe you," the man gasped. "The eyes, the eyes!"

Awkwardly he went down on one knee and took off his tall embroidered cap. "Permit Pheres, merchant and ship owner, to welcome you, my lady and my lord." He hurriedly laid his dagger at their feet. "We need a change of government. The taxes are terrible, and what do we get in return?"

Medea touched his shoulder and said, "Rise, Pheres."

178

He jumped up and began to roar, sending men scurrying to summon other merchants and ship owners, and in between commands he cracked his whip and got the line of hungry men back in order.

That was the way Medea claimed her heritage. There was no bloodshed.

We picked up a considerable procession of people who yelled and sang happily. Most of the Argonauts had caught up with us, leaving a few to guard the ship.

There was a feast that night, and the following day most of the Argonauts set out for their own homes. Ships were always sailing from Corinth to other ports, and the captains were glad to oblige their new rulers by making room for the great adventurers. Besides, the captains were very well paid by these passengers.

Before the lords and princes left, they braced *Argo* with timbers on the sandy shore in the place where they would stay until she fell apart. No one ever sailed in her again.

There was a great sacrifice of bulls to all the gods, with hundreds of the people partaking of the roasted meat and getting a good look at the King and Queen.

When the Argonauts came to say farewell, some of them wept and so did Jason, because they had been through so many perils together. Medea was gracious to each of them, although she had hated them all.

Orpheus kissed my hand and said, "A long life and happiness, little Daphne." My throat filled up, and my tears came so that I could not answer at all.

Touching his hand, I had a terrible foreseeing. His
179

life would be neither long nor happy — although he deserved everything good, because he himself was good.

After the moon had waxed and waned twice, the new government was well established. Medea had learned her lessons well from Arete, Queen of Corcyra. She suggested to Jason what should be done when problems arose, but she did it very subtly, so that he thought the ideas were his own.

Speaking as the hereditary queen, but speaking for Jason who ruled as king, she wisely settled disputes among the people so that few of them ever came to the great public court where Jason was judge. *He* might be impatient, but my lady never was.

Some new tax collectors were appointed, and some new record keepers, and some old ones were retained. The most powerful nobles were invited to councils in the palace — merchants, ship builders, owners of great vineyards and vast olive groves. A few of their daughters were invited to be the Queen's maidens — not because they possessed special skills but because their fathers were influential.

When the government was running as smoothly as a well-built ship before a good breeze, Jason invited a dozen of the nobles to go with him to take the golden fleece to the city of Orchomenus. With their servants, they made a small army. I was glad to see that dirty old sheepskin go, carried on a litter and covered with purple cloth.

Jason dedicated it to the god Ares in the temple in Orchomenus.

The government got along well without him. Everybody got along very well without me, too. I just tried to stay out of the way while I wondered what would happen to me. The serving women in the weaving room were glad of my company, and it was a great relief to have something useful to do with my hands again. The women told me stories about Corinth and asked endless questions about the voyage of *Argo*.

One of Medea's new maidens rushed in breathless one morning to say, "The Queen has asked for Daphne. Who is Daphne?"

"I am Daphne," I said, and she said in surprise, "The way she spoke your name, I thought you were somebody important! She is in her chamber."

Medea stood by a window in the sunshine. She put

both arms around me and kissed me, and I almost cried.

"I want you near me," she said. "Others will be near me too, but that's politics. Wealth is important in Corinth. So you shall have it, to prove that you are the Queen's friend."

"My lady, I'm nobody," I reminded her.

She looked very stern. "Never let me hear you say that again!" she warned.

"I own large properties now, in my own right as my father's daughter. We have record keepers here who draw charts showing boundary lines and remember who owns all the land.

"At the next public court, when my husband comes back, I will transfer some property formally to you, with overseers to take care of it for you."

I curtsied, speechless.

"You might teach these Corinthian girls some manners," Medea suggested. "Rehearse them in settling like doves."

I was afraid she would tell me to teach them some of our dances, but she didn't mention that. She did add, thoughtfully, "Teach them the dream game."

"But my lady," I cried, "I can't — "

"Nonsense!" she snapped, her golden eyes seeming to shoot sparks. "Come here, Daphne." She began to twirl the little golden ball, and by the time she finished murmuring and assuring me, I knew that I could teach them.

So I did, one at a time, and the news spread like wildfire through the city. The dream game became very fashionable. The serving women in the palace begged for it, too, and there was no harm in that.

When Jason came back from Orchomenus, a great reception was held in the palace. He and Medea sat together on a throne of carved stone padded with dyed lamb skins, and the important people of Corinth filed up to them to bow and express their devotion. Medea remarked later, in confidence, that the only thing the Corinthians were *really* devoted to was wealth.

I led Medea's new maidens into the court, and we settled like doves at one side of the throne.

A stately old herald with a fluffy white beard shouted out the names of certain important men of Corinth, calling each one "Companion of the King." This was a new order, Medea's idea. Singling out certain men would insure their loyalty, she told Jason.

After that a few women's names were called, with the title "Companion of the Queen." They came forward singly and curtsied and touched Medea's hand.

Then, to my astonishment, the herald shouted: "Daphne of Colchis!" I walked up and curtsied — and lost my balance and ended kneeling instead of standing.

"The Queen bestows on Daphne certain properties," the herald intoned. He named them, with their boundaries: olive groves, orchards, flocks of sheep and goats and land for grazing them, a house near the city, forest land on which grew timber for building ships, vineyards where the grapes grow that become the famous currants of Corinth. I was trembling.

"And with these properties," the herald intoned, "the Queen in her grace bestows the title of Lady Daphne, *First* Companion to the Queen."

Medea raised me to my feet, and all the people shouted. I went back to her maidens, stumbling because I could not see through the tears.

It was not easy to learn to be Lady Daphne. But it was not impossible, either. Pleasant and patient, thoughtful but strict in the matter of comfort for Medea, neither humble nor haughty — there was much to learn, understanding people and forgetting myself. I could no longer retreat behind the idea that I was nobody important.

Medea's first child, Medeius, a fine boy, was born in the spring. I was seldom allowed to cuddle him, because so many others wanted to, in addition to his own mother. And it was wise to permit the Companions of the Queen to have that privilege. They boasted about it, and Queen Medea was well thought of in Corinth.

One day, crowded out of the nursery by two important landowners' wives and not wanted for anything by anyone, I decided to see whether I had any authority outside the palace. I had not seen anything of the city since that frightening day when Medea unveiled her eyes in the port.

A boy about my age, a page for Jason, was lounging in the courtyard. I summoned him.

"Please tell the captain of the guard that I'd like to speak to him," I said. The boy set off at a run. Immediately the captain marched in, very grand in his body armor and helmet, with his sword and shield clanking.

"Captain, I'd like to visit the port and the shipyards," I said. "How many guards will be needed?"

"No more than myself, my lady," he answered, showing his muscles. "But I'll take six men along for show."

"And I'll take two attendants," I decided.

I went with four, finally, two Companions and one of the maidens and my own serving woman, Althea, whom Medea had given me. The ladies said it wasn't proper to go without a servant. We wore gray robes, suitable for the occasion, and veils because the ladies insisted.

The harbor was full of noise and movement — men pounding and chopping and sawing, men moving loads on their backs and on donkeys and greater loads on wooden rollers, men climbing and tying ropes — and every one of them shouting to someone else.

The captain appointed himself guide.

"Just about the whole world comes to Corinth," he remarked. "You can tell by their clothes and the way they wear their hair which ones are foreigners from far away."

He pointed out the crew of a Phoenician ship and men from Egypt and Libya and cities far to the west and north and men from the islands. Those with fair hair in braids were Hyperboreans, he said, from the land beyond the North Wind.

"Yes, indeed, the whole world comes here," he repeated.

"Do ships ever come from Colchis?" I asked wistfully.

For a moment he acted as if he had never heard of it. "Oh, the Queen's country! It may be, but my duties don't bring me here very often, and I don't know.

"Now there's a ship from the east, you can tell by the pattern of the sails, from very far to the east, beyond the sunrise. And listen to all that noise of heavy wooden rollers — watch now, a ship will come up the hill in a moment. That one is from the west, perhaps from beyond the Gates of Hercules."

Then we saw a wonderful thing, a ship moving without sails and without oars, being pulled by men in rope harnesses. It moved on great rollers that had to be replaced every few feet, those in the back being hauled up to the prow with much shouting of orders.

"We have two harbors here," the captain explained. "Corinth is built on a narrow isthmus. From the west, ships come in through the Gulf. From the east, they come from a bay. There are only four miles of land between the eastern water and the western water. But do you know how far a ship has to sail or row to get from one to the other? Something like two hundred miles! So we simply pull the ships overland and put them into the sea again."

He seemed as pleased with the idea as if he had invented it himself, and it was indeed a wonderful idea, whoever it belonged to originally.

But I was too shocked with sudden understanding to speak.

"Why so silent, little lady?" he asked.

"I was remembering a prophecy, sir. About a place where the world comes from both east and west and ships move untouched by water."

"This must be it," he agreed. "And what is to happen in this place that was prophesied?"

"Why, I am to stay here! That was the prophecy." *And there you will be happy,* poor Mopsus had said.

"Ah, that must be good news to you, little lady," the

captain said, smiling. "For you have traveled far with the Queen, not knowing where you'd come to rest."

We walked on to watch some sweating men who were unloading a ship. Their supervisor seemed very young for so important a job. He carried a small staff of office, to enable strangers to identify him as in charge, but he had no whip.

He did not shout or scold at the workmen; they moved fast and quietly, thinking how to do things the best way, as if they cared. But there was no doubt that the young man was master.

His hair was wavy, dark brown, hanging below his shoulders, so I knew he was not yet eighteen. When he attained manhood he would cut his long hair and dedicate it to Apollo.

One of the ladies with us said sadly, "He is a fine boy, that Myron. See how well the men work for him? But he is not powerful enough to keep what is his, I'm afraid."

The ladies and the captain were glad to tell me about Myron. His father was a rich merchant who had sailed away a year before. No word had come from him since, and his ship was long overdue. He had intended to go only to Crete — a relatively short journey but a dangerous one because of pirates.

The captain shook his head. "He's probably drowned or been taken captive somewhere."

One of the ladies, full of gossip, added, "And the son, Myron, has two jealous uncles who would like to get all the property away from him."

She was a ship builder's wife, and she kept trying to

point out where her husband's men were working, but she really didn't know, because she seldom came to the harbor. She made all kinds of funny mistakes in talking about ships. I didn't embarrass her by calling attention to her errors, of course. I knew more about one ship, at least, than I had ever wanted to learn.

The other lady said, "Lady Daphne, you have strange powers, I've heard. You can see where someone is if you touch something he has touched?"

I answered modestly, "Sometimes."

"Then why don't we ask young Myron if he has something of his father's that you can use in working a spell?"

"It is not a spell. It is just — I don't know what it is. Oh, I don't want to!" I burst out. "What if I see him dead?"

"You wouldn't have to tell the boy," she argued.

The ladies chirped and squeaked in their excitement about this experiment. The captain himself went to speak to Myron. The young man was polite enough, but he did not let anything distract his attention from the work he was overseeing. He glanced toward us, snatched off the embroidered cap he was wearing and handed it to the captain.

Holding it in my hands, I tried to see something. There was nothing at first. Then came the farseeing.

"A big man with a big beard, black with white streaks in it," I said softly. "He is carrying a great load on his powerful shoulders and climbing a landing stage to a ship." I shivered. "He has whip marks on his back."

The captain exclaimed, "Poseidon preserve all sailors! I'll bring the boy over here and you can tell him yourself."

188

Myron stood staring as I told him the farseeing.

"That is my father," he said quietly. "So he is a captive and a slave in some distant port. You don't know where? But he is alive!"

Myron threw back his head and shouted with joy.

"Will you spread the word, my lady?" he implored. "So that everyone will know? Because those who should be my friends are my enemies instead."

"The word will be spread," I assured him. Ah, the buzzing there would be in the palace and all the great houses of Corinth! And in the markets and the port and on the farms!

Myron dropped quickly to his knees and touched the hem of my robe to his lips. I was embarrassed.

He put his cap on his head and said with a broad smile, "This is my lucky cap, and this is my lucky day."

It was my lucky day, too, I thought. He liked me.

189

15

My parents, although very poor, were happy in each other's company, and I had always taken it for granted that other married couples were happy and got along well together. So while Medea's tragedy was budding, to bloom as a frightful flower, I did not notice. She never complained that Jason took long journeys and left the responsibilities of government to her. She was usually in the company of the wives of nobles, and I thought she did not need me.

All sorts of people began to bring me gossip — perhaps to see how I would react.

With a sideways glance, a merchant's daughter or a kitchen boy would tell me what "they" said.

"Of course I don't believe it, but they say the Queen is a witch."

"She knows charms and spells, and she uses them for good. You know how she soothed the pain of the horse-tender whose leg was broken!"

"They say she creates the storms that drown our sailors."

"Only the gods can make storms — and you'd better not let them hear you doubt it!"

"They say she killed her brother."

"She did not! I was with her. She didn't even know he was dead until long afterward. She loved her brother!"

But I could not say, "Jason trapped her brother with a lying promise. Jason killed him." For Jason was King of Corinth. That the people did not admire him was unimportant. They did not fear him, either, except for the unjust decisions he sometimes gave in lawsuits.

"They say Medea smiles when her hands drip with blood at the altar —

"They say she worships a goddess of the barbarians —

"They say she murdered an old king in Jason's country —

"They say Jason caught her holding the baby in the fire to make him immortal —

"They say Jason goes on journeys because he is afraid of the sorcery of the Queen."

What "they" said was sickening, and I could not tell my lady.

They did not say that she tended the sick and eased the dying. They did not say that she had memorized the ancient laws of the city, as recited by the wise old men, and that she gave just decisions when Jason was journeying to other places. She would not let a rich man take a poor man's farm for debt, and so she earned the rich man's anger.

They did not say that she gave the people the only stable government that Corinth had had in two generations, the people prospered, and no enemy stormed the gates.

I worried — but there was nobody I could tell.

191

One day in the fall my steward came to call. He rode in a chariot drawn by mules, with servants running before and after. If he was so rich, how rich was Daphne!

He bowed, smiling, and men began to bring laden carts and donkeys into the courtyard — jars of wine and oil, boxes of currants, bales of wool and leather, bunches of onions and garlic.

"These are samples of the produce of your farms, Lady Daphne," he said proudly. "And I have brought a recorder, famous for his good memory, to tell you of this year's crops." It was wonderful to listen to.

I called for wine and cakes to be served to the steward and the recorder and asked timidly, "Can you find me a small gray donkey, and perhaps a lamb, big enough to leave its mother?"

He was vastly amused. "You could ask for a hundred," he replied.

"One of each is enough. I only want them to amuse the Queen's baby." And to remind me of the flocks my father tended and the donkey I gave my mother.

I kept them in a pen back of the palace. The serving people never understood why I cared for them myself. Little Medeius liked to pet the lamb and ride grandly on the donkey while I held him on.

A few very pleasant things happened. One day when Medea and I were weaving while Medeius slept, a page came in, big-eyed, to say, "Lady Medea, there's a gift for you. Myron the merchant's son brought it — and I never saw anything like it!"

Myron came in, smiling broadly, carrying a light

wooden cage with two lithe, lean, silvery beasts in it. They said loudly, "Yow!" or asked pitifully, "Yow?"

"They are called cats, Lady," Myron explained. "One of my father's captains smuggled them out of Egypt. In that country they are worshipped as gods!"

"Aren't they beautiful!" Medea exclaimed. "Ouch! Thank you, Myron. You have had no news from your father?"

"None, my lady, but I do not give up hope, and the hope that Lady Daphne gave me keeps my uncles afraid."

After he left, Medea remarked, "He's a man now. His hair has been cut."

"He's nice looking, isn't he?" I said innocently.

"He thinks you are, too," Medea said. "He meant the cats for you, of course, but he didn't dare say so. What names will you give them?"

Just then one of them hissed at the other, and the one that had been hissed at slapped the one that had hissed.

"Castor and Polydeuces," I said. "The wrestler and the boxer. The princes from Sparta."

Medea laughed. "One of them is female, but the names will do. Take good care of them. They are very rare beasts."

As the cats grew up they took very good care of themselves, needing little help from anyone. They slept on the softest pillows. They stalked Jason's hunting hounds and made them yelp. Anything they wanted in the kitchens they took. The servants were afraid of them.

Castor and Polydeuces did not remain rare. Polydeuces gave birth to three little cats and went on producing more

193

while the little ones grew up and had their own little cats. As time passed, the Queen's Companions didn't really appreciate receiving another cat as a present, even if the Egyptians did worship them as gods.

I remember a day, when I was seventeen, that was blissfully happy until some news from afar shattered it.

In the morning there was a festival honoring Aphrodite, goddess of love. That was the first year I took part in the procession, carrying garlands and doves with the other girls and women to the temple of the goddess overlooking the Corinthian Gulf.

In the afternoon, when it was over, several in my age group gathered at the home of my friend, Io. That estate had a lovely garden with marble benches and several statues, and the oleander was in bloom. We gathered to rehearse a chorus for the next festival. We didn't do much rehearsing.

I had Medea's older son with me and his official nursemaid.

There were seven of us girls, and eleven young men, some of them the girls' brothers. One of them was nobody's brother. He was Myron, the ship builder's son. His father was safely at home now, and Myron was free of the heavy responsibility he had borne.

The young men's excuse for gathering was to hear about the journey from which one of them had just returned. Having turned eighteen he had gone clear to Delphi for the ceremony of dedicating his hair to Apollo.

The boys flocked together, with bursts of laughter to let us know they were leaving us out of their affairs. We formed our own little group, with our heads bent, and sent our own bursts of laughter to let them know *they* were being shut out.

But naturally the two groups began to mingle. One girl put down her little lap loom to play softly on her brother's lyre, and her brother's friend seized it and said, "Now let me show you what that's supposed to sound like!"

So we made our eyes big with admiration, hearing how a lyre was supposed to sound. Another boy pulled out a shepherd's pipe, but he kept laughing into it and making it squeal.

It was a lovely time there in the shady garden with the oleanders in bloom. I belonged. I was one of them. We all forgot that Daphne was a foreigner with a background different from theirs, a girl different because she was First Companion to the Queen — a girl with no family. Even a little scrubbing maid born of slave parents had family.

The boys talked among themselves — but for us to hear — about the hard schooling they had had. The older ones, with their hair newly shorn, condescended a little to the younger ones. They boasted, laughing, about how many prizes they would win in the Isthmian Games, held in Corinth every two years.

Myron beat his chest and said, "Behold the winner in the four-horse chariot race!" Another boy tripped him, shouting, "I'll show you a chariot race!" He grabbed Myron's feet, and Myron ran on his hands until both fell in a heap.

We laughed and talked and nibbled the fruit brought

out by the serving women. The boys wanted us to rehearse our chorus with the dance that accompanied it,
but we said it was too hot.

They wouldn't admit it was too hot. They did a young
men's dance, with much foot-stamping, while we clapped
the beat. Then they threw themselves on the ground,
dripping sweat and tussling, while we went on with our
handwork and pretended we didn't admire their muscles.

Someone's little brother said, "Let's go for a swim."
The older ones told him to go ahead if he wanted to. He
was only twelve. The big boys wanted to stay where the
girls were.

We talked about everything and nothing. The one
who had been to Delphi had picked up a great deal of
news — the priests there know what is going on everywhere.

"There was a big boar hunt in Calydon," he reported.
"This huge beast was tearing up peasants' huts, and it even
killed some people. So the King invited a lot of heroes
to come and hunt the boar. Most of them were Argonauts."

I could feel embarrassment in the circle of my friends.
They knew I didn't like to talk about that voyage. But
the traveler couldn't very well stop his story then.

"They had a big quarrel before the hunt, because a
woman had been invited. The King's son Meleager
wouldn't let the hunt begin until they agreed to let her
go along. I heard at Delphi that he was the best javelin
thrower in all Greece. But the lady killed the boar, or
Meleager gave her credit for it. Her name is Atalanta.
She's a king's daughter.

196

"Then there was another quarrel, because two of his uncles claimed the credit. And Meleager killed both of them. Did you know him, Daphne? Was he in *Argo*?"

I nodded and went on with my spinning.

He said bluntly, "Meleager's dead now, you know."

I dropped my spindle and stared.

"He was young when he sailed in *Argo*," I said. "About your age. What happened to him?"

"It's a puzzling story. It seems that when he was seven days old, there was a prophecy that he would live only as long as a certain brand that was burning on the hearth. So his mother snatched the brand from the fire and quenched the flame and hid the charred stick away. But the two men he killed were her brothers — so she put the old brand in the fire and let it burn to nothing, and Meleager died."

The girls gasped. Someone murmured, "Her own son! But — her own brothers."

"That Atalanta must be a strange woman," the young man mused.

"She brings disaster," I said.

The boy who had been to Delphi saw that I was upset and close to tears, so he changed the subject — to a worse one. He was a very obtuse young man, always speaking before he did any thinking.

"There was news of a murder up in Thrace," he rattled on. "Some fellow who went around preaching against this new religion of Dionysus — you know, where the women lose their wits and tear up live animals. It's very strong up north. They have even begun to admit the worship to Apollo's temple at Delphi.

"Well, this traveling preacher favored Apollo, and a bunch of Thracian women came at him with clubs and stones and killed him and tore him apart. His head floated to some island, the story goes, and when it was found it was still singing."

He laughed — and I detest him to this day for it — and said, "He could tame lions when he sang, the Delphians told me, or coax forests into marching down mountainsides, but a bunch of wild women killed him."

I threw down my spinning and ran to pick up Medeius so that they wouldn't see my tears. Ah, Orpheus. He knew what his death would be, but he believed that the practices of worshipping Dionysus were savage, so he tried to abolish them.

Now, I thought, he is with his lost Euridice.

198

The gathering broke up soon. I rode my favorite gray donkey, sitting sideways on its back as a lady should. The nursemaid and one of Medea's ladies and little Medeius rode in a light chariot, and Myron walked beside me. He could see that I had been crying.

"Do you sometimes miss all the wonders and excitement of the voyage?" he asked.

"Never!" I said.

"Now that my father is back safe to run the business," he said, "I'm free to go on a voyage or two in one of our merchant ships. I'll probably go to the Land Beyond the North Wind to bring back tin. There is a great demand, of course, because you can't make bronze without it."

My heart sank to my sandals. "Do you have to go so far?" I burst out. He gallantly didn't notice that I had given my thoughts away.

He answered, "But I have never been anywhere. You have been to places you don't even know the names of."

"It wasn't my idea," I said crossly. But remembering that if the Argonauts had not come to Colchis, I would never have come to Corinth where Myron lived, I was cheered.

I moved my arm so that he could see my two bracelets made of amber beads strung on silver wire. Amber is very rare and valuable; it comes from somewhere far to the north.

Myron smiled. "They say that amber is the tears of nymphs who turned into trees."

"It was kind of your father to give me such a present," I said primly. The amber was in fact a gift from his fa-

199

ther, in gratitude for the farseeing that gave Myron strength to go on fighting off his greedy uncles. If Myron himself had brought the gift, I could not have accepted it.

"It's embarrassing," Myron confided, "to be so far behind my age group with my education. But when I had to be at the shipyard every day, I didn't have time to learn the music and history and poetry, or be in the athletic program.

"Now I'm catching up, but it goes slowly. I have private lessons from tutors. The weapons master says I'm progressing. But," he added sadly, "there's something wrong in music. I can't carry a tune. I'll never, never be able to sing."

I leaned toward him and whispered, "You know what? I'll never be able to sing either."

He said indignantly, "Nonsense! You sing like a nightingale."

That was when I knew he loved me.

16

MYRON MADE three voyages before our wedding day. On the third voyage he was not only master of the ship but in charge of trading as well.

Myron's father had suffered greatly during his captivity, and his health was never good after he returned.

I learned what most girls have to learn sometime: how to wait for the return of a dear one. And there was something I knew without learning: When Myron told tales of his perilous adventures, I should not remind him that I had had perilous adventures, too.

For the wedding, my own house was decked and garnished, and I lived there for a few days with six of my girl friends, because the wedding should be from the bride's home, and the palace was not a happy place any more.

Medea carried the great bridal torch for me, as I had for her. Jason was not there, although she had humiliated herself by asking him to postpone one of his frequent journeys. He had gone with a retinue of servants and some young noblemen to Aetolia, where Atalanta now lived with her father Iasus and her mother Clymene.

Because I had no relatives, Medea placed my hand in Myron's as we faced the hearth in the largest room of my house. The chief priest of Poseidon sacrificed for us.

Then Medea kissed me and raised her voice in the marriage song. My husband and I rode to his house in a litter carried by his friends. His father was not well enough to help carry it. He walked beside us.

Medea's two sons walked ahead of the litter for a short distance, waving leafy branches and joining their piping voices in the hymn. Mermerus was only a toddler, so his nurse soon snatched him up and praised him, and one of the ladies took Medeius out of the procession when he began to tire.

After Jason returned from his journey, Myron and his father and I were summoned to the palace for a social gathering. Jason told with amusement what had happened in Aetolia.

"Atalanta — that fighting girl who stowed away on *Argo*, you know — was finally accepted by her father. The first thing he did when she joined his household was to start looking for a husband for her."

I gasped. Not only was Atalanta vowed to the virgin huntress, Artemis, sister of Apollo, but she had been warned by Apollo's own oracle at Delphi that she must never marry.

Jason continued: "She held out against her father's command for a while, and then she gave in. She said she would marry the man who could defeat her in a foot race — and any man who lost the race to her, she would kill."

Jason's whole audience gasped at that, and someone asked the obvious question: "Did she do it?"

Jason shrugged. "Oh, yes, three or four times. I don't remember their names. That happened before I got there. She is so swift of foot that she reached the goal with time to pick up her bow and fit an arrow to it and shoot the man who gambled on winning her and her father's kingdom.

"But when I was there, she met her match. Melanion of Arcadia fooled her.

"He had three little golden apples — real gold — in his hand when the race began, and he tossed them ahead of Atalanta, one at a time. While he raced past her, she swerved and bent to pick them up. So he won the girl for his wife. I stayed for the wedding."

Medea asked gently, "Has she been released, somehow, from her vow to Artemis?"

Jason shrugged. "I didn't ask. She and her bridegroom had gone on a hunting trip when I left there."

Stories about the mystery of Atalanta still drift in to Corinth. One of them is that she and Melanion were turned into lions as punishment. Anyway, nobody has seen her since that hunting trip.

One of the palace guests asked, fawning, "Lord Jason, are you planning another journey?"

"Oh, yes. Up to Thebes to talk to King Creon about a treaty." He glanced at Medea, but she seemed not to notice.

After we got home, Myron said with a frown, "Corinth needs no treaty with the Theban king. Our borders do not touch. Jason has been up there twice in two years. What attracts him?"

Myron was far away from Corinth, on his fourth voyage, when the news came down from Thebes. Myron's father was growing weaker; he spent much time on his couch. He was resting against cushions in the shade in the courtyard when one of his captains hurried in to tell him:

"They say that Jason is going to marry the daughter of Creon of Thebes!"

"Nonsense. He is married to Medea," the old man replied.

"They say there was something strange about that wedding. Only a threat made Jason marry her. They say the marriage is no marriage here."

"The King and Queen of Corcyra were witnesses to it!" I protested.

Myron's father spoke gently to me: "There is sailors' gossip that you never hear, daughter. They say that Jason has spread the suspicion that the regent here did not die of natural causes. They say Medea poisoned him."

"But he died before *Argo* landed in Corinth — she never saw him in her life!"

The captain looked at me with pity — he was a rough, fierce fellow, but he knew what pity was.

"The Queen is a witch, they say. She can cast spells from afar."

I gulped. "I must ask Myron what to do. Where is his ship now, do you think?"

"If all went well, and if this wind holds, he should be here in a few days."

"I must tell Medea, or be with her when she gets the news."

The captain took a deep breath and blurted out, "She has it. Jason's messenger went first to her."

The sick old man raised a hand. "Take a guard with torches to light Daphne's way to her lady."

Medea was pacing in her chamber when I ran in. The children were asleep, their nurse cowering in a corner. Medea faced me with a smile, and I knew she was afraid.

"The boys and I must leave the palace," Medea said calmly. "We must leave, King Jason says, when the Theban girl comes. The Princess Glauke, Jason's bride."

"To my home and Myron's, of course."

"No, not there. But perhaps to the house I gave you? I have nothing of my own. It is all Jason's now. By the decision of the great judge Jason!" She laughed wildly.

"The house is yours, and everything else you gave me. But will you be safe there?"

"What difference does that make? I have nothing to live for except my children. Medeius will rule Corinth when Jason dies, even if the Theban girl gives him other children."

She laughed shrilly. "And I know how he will die! Ah, I know. I have foreseen his death.

"*Argo* will kill him, *Argo* the ship. He goes often to sit with *Argo*, dreaming of the past, boasting to his attendants. He sits under the prow, there on the shore. Some day the prow will fall and crush him.

"But before that," she intoned like one who prophesies, "he will wander from city to city, childless and wifeless, hated by all men!"

205

"And where will you be, my lady?"

"What does it matter?"

"Your sons matter."

She stopped pacing and looked far away with burning, golden eyes.

"There is an ancient shrine to Hecate on the island of — never mind the name of the island," she said softly. "I ordered it rebuilt a year ago. It is the house of the Dark Goddess, needing only to be reconsecrated. The people there would defend Hecate's priestess.

"And what command will come next from Lord Jason, I wonder? I will not leave this house until he himself tells me to go!"

She stayed in the palace, holding her head high, keeping her household in order as she always had — but few servants were left now that I had known. New ones had come in, Jason's creatures. Medea did not sit as judge in lawsuits now. There were none. People who disagreed fought instead of asking for justice. And there were no more little groups of the sick and injured asking for her help.

The next command came by messenger three days after the first one:

"The Lord Jason requires that Medea of Colchis send his bride a splendid gift. It must be the fine enchanted robe that Medea brought from Colchis in the ship *Argo*."

The messenger trembled as he spoke, they say. From that day he sickened, and before the year was finished, he died. They say he was burned by the fire in her eyes.

"Ah, yes," Medea answered calmly. "I will show you where it is kept, and you may take the whole chest. But remember, I have never touched the robe. It is very rich and beautiful, but there is said to be a spell on it. It may be dangerous to touch."

"That is what Lord Jason said you would say, being unwilling to send his bride the gift."

She laughed lightly. "Why should I be unwilling to give her the robe when she has already claimed my husband? I never wanted the robe."

When Myron's father heard about that (and everyone heard about it; my lady had no privacy any more) he remarked, "Jason is playing with her the way the Egyptian cats play with a crippled bird."

Medea chatted lightly when I went to see her. So did I, because of the listeners.

"They say Jason's bride is a pretty thing and very young," she said. "They are married already, and he will bring her to Corinth soon."

How little it seemed to matter to Medea! But there were servants in the room, and I was not sure whether two of them were loyal to her. They were probably Jason's spies.

"You have had another messenger?" I asked.

"A new one almost every day, with additional news or commands from Jason. Of course I'm doing everything he wants done."

"It is a tiring journey from Thebes, I suppose?"

"It must be — partly by land and partly by water. But of course she'll have all the comforts. More than we had, my dear." She chuckled.

"I don't ever want to go on another journey!" she said — and closed her eyes as she said it.

That silent signal was unseen by the watchers in the room. I guessed its meaning: *I am lying. Find me a ship!*

With her arm linked in mine, she walked with me to the gate, chatting and smiling, the very picture of a contented woman who had never heard of jealousy, who had never been the victim of selfish cruelty.

One of Jason's spies walked, listening, close behind us.

Medea said cheerfully, "Just today I was remembering the game we played in the meadow. You learned it very well at last, almost as well as my sister. We must play it again soon, my friend and helper."

She kissed my cheek and waved good-by, smiling. She was very calm — and terribly afraid.

I hurried to Myron's father and told him, "Medea is in danger! What can I do? What can I do to help her?"

"I'll get the shipyard captain in here," he decided instantly, and summoned a runner. "We must set up a system for getting information."

The captain was a grim man who thought fast.

"I know where Jason's messengers touch shore after they cross the Gulf in little boats," he said. "They're fast runners, but they're mortal men. They tire. We'll send mounted messengers to ride back in relays, bringing the news to me ahead of them."

"Not to the Queen?" I asked timidly.

"I'll get it to the Queen," he promised. "And nobody else in the palace will know it."

"But how will your messengers get it from Jason's runners?"

"Everybody in the sailors' tavern up there learns everything in a hurry," he answered with a sour smile.

One morning while I waited for Myron's ship — pacing, not spinning, forgetting to eat, unable to sleep — the worst message of all came on the lips of a breathless rider on a sweating horse:

"Princess Glauke of Thebes is dead of a frightful fever — she died within a day after putting on the robe that was a gift from Medea and her sons.

"Jason is raging with grief and fury. He will cast the witch out of the kingdom, and she will never see her children again. He is on his way — he will be in Corinth tomorrow!"

At noon, a sailor from the port brought us a message: "A ship has been sighted from Aegina. A flashing signal there sent the word. It is probably Myron's ship — no other is expected."

Myron's ship was beached when the sun was low in the west. I was waiting at the landing stage, clothed in black so that he would know there was trouble.

"You must take Medea and her boys away tonight," I gasped. "To an island she knows but will not name to me."

He spoke over his shoulder: "Don't unload. Be ready to sail again."

I told him briefly what had happened. He grasped the situation at once.

"Are some of the servants loyal to her?" he asked.

"A few would risk something for her, I think."

"And perhaps some people outside the palace."

"Perhaps. Those whose pain or sickness she has eased."

"And those who appreciate her because she gave them just decisions. Now here is what we will do — "

Yes, there were loyal people who risked their lives. The horsetender and his daughter brought the younger of Medea's two boys to the temple of the Healing Apollo, bandaged with rags as if he had been burned, all three of them crying.

From the temple, two of my serving women brought him in a basket, of the kind used for burying dead children, to a shed on the waterfront. He lay still as death, because of a potion his mother had sent with him.

But Medeius, the older boy, they had not been able to bring out of the palace.

They say — they say — the friends of Medea whispered aghast. The word spread to her enemies — the witch from Colchis is working an evil spell on Jason and his house, his sons!

She has threatened to kill the children! The robe they sent to Thebes killed Jason's bride, you know. Hurry, hurry!

They hurried, hither and yon, without leadership in the confusion. They were like ants when the ant hill is disturbed, but ants know what to do. The enemies of Medea did not. A few ran to the palace, but most ran away from it.

That was vital: terror. Those who are frightened are more easily convinced. In the field where Jason fought the fire-breathing bulls and mowed down the Sown Men with his swinging sword, even the suspicious, fearless Argonauts had fallen, writhing, when fear convinced them.

In the courtyard of the palace Medea's friends protected her while she began her sorcery — the armed men stood with their backs to her so that they could withstand the spell for a little while.

Until I slipped in through a doorway from the kitchen (and I saw two dead men, for there had been fighting), Medea glided and chanted alone.

The fire leaped and smoked. I heard her from far off, shrieking, "Hecate! Dark Goddess, come!"

I knew what to do. At first nobody noticed me, clothed in black, and then everyone saw me, and a groan went up: "There are two witches now!"

A great gong was ready by the hearth where the flames leaped and a club to strike it with and the ivory box of herbs.

Medea was majestic and terrible. She wore a very tall headdress of carved ivory, with the skulls of small animals set on spikes and above them a crescent moon. Around her eyes she had painted red coloring. In one hand she carried a long staff, and in the other, the brass sandal of the Dark Goddess.

She screamed, "Come, Hecate!" and I struck the great gong. The sound was not so much a sound as a shudder in the blood and in the bones.

"Watch the sandal! Watch the sandal!" she commanded, holding it high so that the light flickered on it.

I cried, "Come, Hecate!" and scattered herbs on the fire. A great stench arose.

"Watch the sandal! It is changing!" she chanted. "It is a serpent — see how it writhes!"

The terrorized people in the courtyard, friends and enemies alike, groaned and bowed and howled, "Hecate! Hecate!"

211

"There she rides down the sky! Hecate! Hecate!

"In the chariot drawn by serpents! Hecate! Hecate!

"On your faces, mortals! Here is Hecate!"

Medea was gliding no longer. She leaped and motioned with the long staff, and the people melted away before her and fell on their faces.

Then we were through the door, and they were still howling, seeing Hecate, as we ran.

It was horror unforgettable. I too saw Hecate riding down the sky! I saw Medea standing in the serpent chariot with a bloody sword in her hand, shrieking with

triumphant laughter, with the dead bodies of her two children. I saw the chariot fly off into the dark sky, because that was what she told us we were seeing.

We fled. We dodged. We raced out through the kitchens.

Myron was where he had promised to be. He said, "Medea, carry this. Daphne, take this."

And the howling went on as we fled into the dark street.

My burden was a clay jar in a coarse net to carry it with. I was trembling so much that I could hardly hold it.

Medea carried a tub of stinking fish.

Myron's back was bent under a bundle that might have had a young calf in it.

We met frantic people running toward the palace. If they carried torches, we scuttled and sneaked and did not answer questions. Nobody paid much attention to three kitchen servants who acted guilty because they were stealing a few things from the palace!

At the gate of the shipyard, armed seamen parted to let us through and then stood shoulder to shoulder again, with clubs and spears. But no one was following yet.

I dropped my jar with a crash, and Medea tossed aside the tub of fish. Myron pulled his precious burden from the big sack — no stolen calf, but Medea's older son, Medeius, gasping but making no outcry.

Myron snatched up the boy — he was too cramped to run — and we fled toward the small torch that marked the landing stage.

When Medea was at the top of the landing stage, she

turned and whispered, "This is the only gift I have for you — a blessing from the goddess who gives and withholds — "

There was a sharp command, and we were parted forever. A seaman hastily passed my lady down into the wooden pit. Myron seized me around the waist with one arm and leaped down into the shallow water.

The vessel moved out into night and danger on the tossing sea.

They say her evil spell killed Glauke of Thebes. They say that in her rage she murdered her own little boys so that Jason would grieve beyond comforting, childless and friendless.

But the boys are with her on an island somewhere in the sea.

Jason travels from city to city, abhorred by all men because of the curse they say his wife cast on him, although nobody can remember hearing her curse him. When he is in Corinth, he sits often under the prow of *Argo*, which is bleaching and rotting on the shore.

On another night, our ship slipped quietly back into its landing place. The captain came to tell me the blessing of Medea:

"The priestess of Hecate prays that Myron's wife will never learn what hatred is."

AUTHOR'S NOTE

THE STORY of the legendary Medea has entranced readers for more than twenty-five centuries. Before it was ever written down, it must have been told in poetry by men who sang it to a musical accompaniment played on a harp.

There are many versions of Medea's tragic story. Most of them say she was a dreadful person. Medea had strange powers; people feared her and told terrible stories about her. But since she was imaginary in the first place, I have as good a right as anyone to tell about her as I think she must have been.

It's hard to decide which is the "true" version of a legend when nothing at all in the story can be proved true. There are inconsistencies in the legendary Quest of the Golden Fleece and the tragedy of Medea. Ancient writers didn't even agree on the passenger list of the good ship *Argo*. Most of them didn't mention Atalanta as one of the crew. I'm sure the Argonauts wouldn't have taken her along willingly, so she must have been a stowaway.

Another inconsistency in the legend is the home city of the unfortunate Princess Glauke. Some writers say she lived in Corinth; some say she lived in Thebes. In the ruins of ancient Corinth there is still a spring named for her.

The story of Medea has been told many, many times. The oldest version that remains to us is, strangely enough, the one known to most people now. That is a play, *Medea*, by the Greek tragic playwright Euripides, who was born 485 years before the birth of Christ and lived in Athens. Euripides' *Medea* is sometimes produced on the stage even in our time. In that play she rides off through the air in a chariot drawn by dragons, carrying the dead bodies of her children. But you and I know that's not what *really* happened.

One thing all the storytellers agree on is that Prince Jason, whom she loved and helped and married, treated her abominably. He tired of her, decided to marry another princess, and said that Medea was not really his wife.

These things are supposed to have happened more than three thousand years ago — a generation before the fall of legendary Troy. A form of writing existed elsewhere in the world, but writing was not yet known in Greece. Money had not yet been invented. Travel was very dangerous, and foreigners were under suspicion everywhere.

Colchis was at the eastern end of the Black Sea in what is now the Soviet Republic of Georgia. Corinth is in Greece, and a canal now enables ships to pass from the gulf to the bay. Long ago, they really were hauled overland across the isthmus.

If you have read Homer's magnificent stories, the *Iliad* and the *Odyssey*, you have met some of the people mentioned in this book. The *Iliad* concerns the anger of Achilles, great fighting hero of the Greeks, who is mentioned here as the baby son of Peleus and a sea goddess. The hero of the *Odyssey*, Odysseus — but we speak of him more often as Ulysses — visited the island of Corcyra long after the Argonauts did. He was rescued by Princess Nausicaa, who is a baby in this book.

Odysseus, like the Argonauts, passed the Sirens' Isle, and like them he visited the nymph Circe — he stayed on her island for a whole year.